THE POP SONGS OF CLUBLAND

STEVEN CAGNINA

1

FEBRUARY 21, 1994

It's fun to think about a girl you're not supposed to think about.

Ansley picks up an album by a band no one has heard of: Tito Revelations. He takes out the vinyl and examines the grooves. Life is a lot like this vinyl. Rites of passage separated into tracks. Today is his birthday – not that he told anyone, and Ansley figures he's starting the 24th album of his life tonight.

Every album has songs about girls, and Ansley thinks of girls as pop songs. Beautiful catchy things that can break your heart. Right now he is thinking of a pop song called Connery. And thinking about her is making him think about his life and how much longer he can sustain it.

The life Ansley has now started in the summer of 1992. That's when Ansley, a cocky kid from nowhere, bought an abandoned horseshoe shaped collection of buildings. The open end of The Horseshoe, as the locals call it, faces the ocean. That was a big selling point when the place was built, since the buildings were originally small hotels which sat on top of restaurants and tourist businesses. But that was back in the 30's. By the 70's the hotels had become decrepit and the businesses below them had closed. Eventually the hotels couldn't get anyone to stay in them, even with cheap rates and close beach proximity. For twenty years The Horseshoe stood as a local curiosity. People would say, Gosh I thought they tore that down.

Many a developer in the 80's had looked for the owner. His name was listed as Benton Practice. No one could find him. The taxes were paid yearly by an overseas corporation, which itself was a mystery. So prime beach real estate went nowhere. And then two years ago a kid named Ansley bought it. He showed up with a renovation crew. His idea: Take the small, cozy four-story hotels and turn them into giant nightclubs. And now two years later, The Horseshoe is the center of all social life in the state. But this did not come about without blackmail, pissed off organized crime, politics, and the strange will of Ansley.

He refuses to sell any part of the property. The club runners don't like being leasers in such a lucrative enterprise and their criminal ties are usually enough to fix such business interests. But that's where the blackmail comes in. And Ansley's otherworldly connections.

Ansley kept the spaces the old hotels sat on as separate businesses, which also pisses off the club runners. They want to use the spaces to open their own side businesses or just expand their nightclubs. Instead Ansley has allowed people who can't make it in life to open whatever nutty business they want. One lady sells nothing but turtle decorations. One guy runs a cobbler shop. A lot run restaurants or cafes, which do make a lot of money, even during the daytime. But they're all run by nuts. And their profits are helped greatly by Ansley not charging them rent. The Horseshoe has turned into a strange collection of crooked people, beautiful people, and outcasts who accidentally got in thanks to Ansley.

THE HORSESHOE IS ALSO CALLED Clubland. That is the official name Ansley gave it.

Clubland is only two exits from the state capital. And so politics is also a part of the nightlife. On Clubland's car-less street you can taste the power and ecstasy and cocaine and sex and sweat. The car-less part is a big deal. In a brilliant business move Ansley built a large parking garage a half mile from The Horseshoe. There is no other bulk parking near. The parking biz is a lot like the cemetery biz, except you can resell the plots as many times as you like. And Ansley's underhanded ways has kept any parking competition away.

Why an orphan named Ansley would create or want all this no one knows. They don't know he's an orphan, they don't know where he got the money to buy and develop The Horseshoe. They don't know a damn thing about him. They figure his real name probably ain't Ansley either. But one of his enemies is hoping the murder that happened on Friday night will bring him down.

A senator's son overdosed; but the autopsy said he had been poisoned. The dead kid was 22 and put bluntly, an asshole. A privileged Ivy Leaguer who never worked a day in his useless life. But his death has thrown a spotlight on Clubland and the press want comments from its owner. The police want to talk to him, too. Ansley knows he is being setup. But none of this is on his mind right now. Right now he thinks only of the pop song Connery O'Hara. A five foot three Irish girl from Ohio named after the best James Bond. Ansley has decided that Connery has a lot of problems and much to the chagrin of Ansley's two direct employees, Randy and Jen, he's intent on solving them.

Connery is also the girlfriend, at least she was until last week, of Alex Pacheco. A club runner, drug dealer, and the guy trying to frame Ansley for the murder of the senator's kid.

Alex spends all his free time trying to find a way around Ansley's "dead man switch." Ansley has told all the club runners that if something bad happens to him, their dirt will be dumped. So this frame is a risky bet for Alex. But it's worth the risk because of his hatred for Ansley.

Another club leaser last year let his hate get the best of him. Shivers and Shakes club runner Robert Johnson made a move against Ansley. He called Ansley's bluff. That was his first mistake. His second was his assassin missed.

Within 24 hours the FBI had raided his home and his wife had filed for divorce. He swore revenge. But things have a way of working out. In prison, he died. They never decided how. They never bothered with why. And since Ansley lived, his enemies still didn't know if the dead man switch is real.

Ansley is thinking about none of this right now. He's thinking about what he should wear on his date tonight with Connery. A date that will motivate Alex even more to frame him for murder. It's a Monday. But every day is Friday in Clubland and Fridays are for burning. So lets see what I can burn tonight, Ansley thinks.

2

THE STASIS OF THE SWEET BARTENDER GIRL

Connery and Ansley are sitting at Cafe Bob's. A coffee shop which sits under Alex Pacheco's Club Stations. Ansley picked the place. And he's wrapped up in a thought.

Finally he blurts the thought out, "You know earlier tonight before I got here, I had this thought: That my life – maybe your life – is like an album. We have one for each year – or maybe it's divided into eras. Like tonight – tonight being here with you feels like Track One of a new album of my life. And girls are pop songs to me. I meet a pretty girl and I always think about what kind of pop song she is. And Connery – you're a very pretty girl."

"I am confused. Am I an album or a pop song?"

"Whether you're an album or not is up to you. But you're definitely a pop song on my album."

"This doesn't sound that cool."

"You haven't heard the song yet." Ansley smiles as he changes the subject, "How former of a girlfriend are you to Alex?"

He studies Connery's face now for any deception. This isn't particular to her – he does this to everyone. His two employees, Randy and Jen, are the closest things to a friend he has and they always feel "studied" by him.

Randy and Jen have a lot of affection for Ansley because he helped both of them recover. Randy had been a senator's chief of staff in 1989. A chubby, agreeable boy wonder of politics. But he got caught in a gay sex scandal. The 80's were not a good decade to be gay. And so he was banished from Washington.

Jen is beautiful, blonde, freckled and bipolar. That last one has destroyed her life many times over already and she's only 22. Randy waited till 26 to destroy his life.

Both are loyal to Ansley. He's a great boss. But the orphan in him trusts no one.

Yet for some reason he is drawn to Connery. Ansley has only loved one girl; she never let herself love him because he was poor. Even though he has money now he doesn't seek her out, because he can't forgive her for not overlooking his poverty.

As the de facto leader and Mystery Man of Clubland, Ansley gets with a lot of bartenders and waitresses. But he never stays with anyone.

Connery works as a bartender for a rival club of Alex's, Pink Lucid. The club goers and staff were amazed the other night when Ansley sat at Connery's bar and ordered several Dickel neat with a beer chaser. Ansley never drinks in Clubland. His lack of drugs and booze while cruising all the clubs has become legendary. And everyone noticed the girl he was making the exception for. It took about two seconds for the news to reach Alex.

Connery steadies her brown eyes on Ansley now and says, "How former am I? I told you the other night at Lucid that Alex and me sort of broke up a few days ago. I had just met you and you started in on Alex and me!"

"I thought we had met before the other night."

"No. You never stopped by my bar. I knew of you – but everybody in The Horseshoe knows who you are."

Connery has a button nose and faultless Irish skin, both of which Ansley has been admiring since they sat down. She is squeezed uncomfortably in a tight blue dress. She prefers to dress down and he can tell she doesn't like this Club Girl outfit. Her brownish hair is worn up. She seems to prefer it that way. But Ansley is imagining it falling down softly on her shoulders.

Connery's innate cuteness and simple worldview can't hide a sadness that's traced around her. She has an ominous aura that Ansley can't define. It would be a lot easier if I could just ask her where this bad aura came from, he thinks. But they never let you just ask.

ANSLEY SIPS HIS BEER. Connery sips her tequila.

"So tell me how much does Alex hate me?"

"A lot man. But you seem like a good human. Everyone besides the club runners loves you. Can I ask you something?"

Ansley watches her brown eyes dart around. She has a short attention span. It isn't because of shallowness. Probably just modern life caused it. Her eyes finally land on him and she asks, "How did you get the money to own all this? Were your parents rich?"

"Who knows. They didn't tell me." Ansley smiles but it isn't friendly, more evasive. "How old are you?"

"29."

This shocks Ansley. She looks 19!

"How the hell did you end up here at 29?"

"When you asked me out tonight I asked around about you. I know a lot of the girls you've been with. I am not looking for anything but friendship right now. If that's ok."

"Well darlin' that's all I was looking for –" He can't finish this crap without laughing. "I can't say that shit straight. No man is looking to just shake hands with a pretty girl Connery. And you are a pretty girl. Even when you're dressing down baby you can't hurt the goods."

He smiles and this time it is friendly. "So what did the 'gals' say about me? I'm cute? Wonderful? Attentive in bed? Paid for their grandmother's retirement community?"

"They said you're cool. Very cool man. And you like to listen to them talk about shit. They said you're kinda like a therapist."

"And I gather you've never wanted to date your therapist?"

"Never had a therapist and no thanks man."

Her voice has a husky girlishness to it; it's charming the way it wraps around a word like *man*.

"I dated mine last year," Ansley says. "It was very Freudian of me."

"What's *Freudian*?" Connery doesn't like his smirk at her not knowing who Freud is. "I don't know things man. Ok! Like trivia and shit. So suck a dick if that bothers you."

"I'm not bothered by your ignorance."

"Fuck you man!"

"Two truths I live by Connery: Classy has nothing to do with money. And smart has nothing to do with knowing facts."

When Connery's interest is piqued, her attention span problems fade away. Ansley would be surprised to see how much she is seeing in his blue eyes. She has a high level of emotional intelligence. She trusts her gut. From the moment Ansley spoke to her the other night at the bar she trusted him. Kindness is a thing that, unlike other girls, she finds attractive, not boring. She is sure that Ansley is kinder than he wants to admit. But all the stuff she heard about him wasn't great. A few girls said they'd seen his temper and in those hot moments, he wasn't the same person. That didn't scare Connery, but the look in those girls' eyes as they recounted seeing Ansley angry did. Only a real darkness could scare them like that.

"Why did you accept my invite to this cafe?" Ansley asks. "You know it's right below Alex's club. You wanna piss him off?"

"No. I wanna know why you want to."

"Alex is a bad dude."

"Yeah. He's not a good human. Mostly anyway."

"Why did you hook up with him?"

"I met him after my dad died. Three years ago. We moved out here a year ago when you rented him this club. He was there for me when my dad died."

"Where's your mother?"

"They were divorced. My mother is needy. I had to be there for her. For every fucking thing."

Ansley can see that her mother/daughter relationship is reversed. Having to be the Mom in that relationship is one trauma that can't be healed. The best she could do is put geography between them.

"So your dad was the best parent?"

"He taught me how to be the human I am." Her eyes are getting misty.

"Sorry. I don't mean to make you cry."

"No I still can't help it. But I wanna talk about him. I don't want him to be a sad thing you know?"

Ansley nods. He gets it. If he had a dad he is sure what's in her eyes now – loss and love and an emptiness that will never fade, would be in his.

"So why Alex?"

"Because he was there for me."

"That simple."

"That simple."

"You want my opinion?"

"Probably not. But ok."

"It sounds to me like he was just *there* and you added the 'for you' part. You don't expect much do you? That's a fault. Where did you meet my buddy Alex anyway?"

"Where else – a bar. He's not all bad. But he just is. With Alex I never think about the future. I never have to think."

"Why did you get a job recently at Pink?"

"Because it pays a lot in tips! Da!"

"And it gives you financial independence. And you're tired of *not* thinking about Alex. You have trouble leaving things don't you?"

"I don't handle change well. Dad didn't either."

"It's been a tough month for you. You got a new job and lost an old boyfriend."

"Kind of lost."

Ansley's hyper focus launches in. "You seem pretty fucking wishy washy on that. So what the fuck are you guys?"

"We're not anything man. Mostly. It's just one of those things that's been going on."

"But you're something *kind of lost*?"

"It's all fucked up man, ok? I'd rather not talk about this shit."

We're going to need a lot of booze, Ansley thinks.

"Let's get out of here," he says.

"Well what club do you wanna go to?"

"Fuck clubs. I hate clubs."

"But you own Clubland."

"I owned a Chevette once. I hated it too. I am gonna take you somewhere special. To me anyway."

No one in Clubland would come to a place like Seashells. It is a dive bar that dove and never came up. Nothing in it has been fixed or replaced in decades. The bathrooms are years of bodily fluids hastily bleached over. The food has one taste: Greasy. At some point in an alcoholic's life, a dive like Seashells becomes the only place that makes sense. And Ansley is, if not an alcoholic, an enthusiastic drinker. He prefers dark dives with Leonard Skynyrd playing on the jukebox and faces made of smoke and wrinkles.

Connery is a big drinker. For a little girl she can hold her own. And she loves a place like Seashells. She's never been into trendy nightclubs. Connery prefers simple to audacious and cheap to overpriced.

Ansley doesn't broach anything new until drink three. A true test of any relationship is whether you can say nothing and feel zero pressure. He is relieved that Connery is ok in silence and people watching. But the universe doesn't let Connery just sit quietly in a bar. Ansley doesn't know how it happened, but by drink two Connery is talking with the regulars and good friends with the bartender, a saucy broad in her 40's with big breasts and a thick ass. Within a half hour she is the most popular chick in the place.

The girl that rejected Ansley because he was a poverty case, she had this quality too. Boys and girls in the crowd instinctively liked her. Except she fit nicely into a debutante air. She went with higher education and fancy restaurants and Porsches.

Connery is not interested in that crap. She isn't a girl that wants fancy parties and rich husbands – although Alex has money (not as much as he likes to portray though).

As Ansley watches Connery effortlessly make friends it occurs to him that unlike his lost girl, Connery actually sees others. With his lost girl, people were only a reflection of herself. But Connery is different, kinder. Sure she's sharp enough to cut you if you get out of line, but there's an empathy for human misery that you either have in your heart or you don't and she's got it. It makes sense, Ansley thinks, she is a bartender. Therapist or bartender are the best jobs for her.

During drink three he manages to corral her into a quieter corner.

"You're a cool chick babydoll," he says.

Grinning, "You seem surprised?"

"I am always surprised when I am not bored. I sound like an asshole huh?"

"I think you are kind of an asshole. But a cool one. You're a good human."

"So you're not broken up with Alex?"

"You really want to talk about him huh."

"Have you ever told him you love him?"

"We've been together for a while. Yeah."

"I wonder."

"You wonder what?"

"If when you said love you just meant a familiar contempt that doesn't threaten you." He takes a big sip. "You want kids in life?"

"Not with Alex!"

"Huh."

Connery does not like the face he makes.

"So what does that face mean. Are you judging me?"

"29 ain't the end but it's the end of the beginning when it comes to kids. You don't have all the time in the world baby."

"I know. It's just –"

"He's *there*. And he will always be *there* enough to be *there*." Ansley leans closer to her, her lips damp and near. "I am sitting here all night talking to a pretty girl and I am not thinking of hitting on her. Rather, I am thinking of stasis. What is it you want Connery? In ten years? Twenty?"

"I don't know. God those girls are right. You are a therapist. What do *you* want Ansley?"

"I have no idea. So in that way we are alike. You know I think the world fucks people like us over. We're not meant to be in the system. I seem to have beaten it. But I really haven't."

His emotions are boiling over now – alcohol and repressed sentiment will do that to you. "I think you belong on a small farm with animals and kids everywhere."

"That sounds really nice actually."

"*Does it?*" He nods to himself. "Does it now Connery...."

Connery studies him again. His whole self has fallen into some thought too sad to mention and too sad to hide. "Did any of those Clubland girls ever ask you any questions?"

Smiling, "No. No they never do. Girls like to be the focus. They like to be understood by a man. Known by a man. As long you don't really know and understand them."

"Well what if I ask you a few questions. Will you answer them?"

Her eyes hold his. It is never a good idea to break a precedent that protects your heart. But then again, fuck it. "Ask."

"How did you buy Clubland?"

"An eccentric rich guy named Benton Practice sold it to me for one dollar. He wasn't meant to be in the system either. We hated the world in the same ways. And he liked to drink in places like this. I was in Ohio at the time. Freezing my ass off. And I am drinking whiskey in some dive like this one and we start chatting. I told him I was an orphan –"

"You're an orphan!"

"Yeah. It's not very interesting."

"But have you ever talked to your real parents? Did you grow up in a shelter or foster home or did someone adopt you –"

"*Connery*! Focus! I know you have attention deficit issues. But focus!"

"Sorry man. I just find it sad you're an orphan."

"I know. It's why I don't tell anyone. And I am trusting you not to tell anyone. Out of necessity I am making you my therapist for the rest of the night. And as my therapist you're bound to secrecy. Go get us more drinks and I'll finish my story."

"So Benton gave me Clubland. Why he owned it who knows. He put some millions in a dummy corporation I could use to start renovations. And he set me up with a finance guy."

"All this because you bonded over alcohol?"

Raising his drink, "This stuff does solve so many things it breaks!"

"Is he proud of you?"

"He's dead."

Connery looks for pain in Ansley's expression but he gives none. His eyes stay on her.

"Benton was a weird good dude," he says. "Anyway he put me in touch with all kinds of people. Especially people in government and law enforcement. I couldn't understand why but when I was setting up Clubland I found out why. You see these nightclubs – they are the juice that drives all the corruption and power. People make all that cash so they can spend it at a place like Clubland. They come in made and go out broken. Sex and drugs make people vulnerable and all people want is to be high when getting off on their kink. You get me?"

"I don't think I get everything you mean now."

"Blackmail isn't about deeds. It's about the heart and soul's needs. And if those needs are prohibited, cha-ching! The world works off leverage baby. But there's something darker going on recently. Something I don't understand."

"The murder?"

Ansley shakes that question off. "If you could go anywhere Connery where would it be?"

Grinning, "Where they have farms."

"Yeah. Some place quiet."

"I want life to slow down."

"How fast is it going tonight?"

Connery touches his hand. "It's going ok," she says.

LATER THEY ARE WALKING on the beach. It is 5am. Ansley wants to kiss her small lips and lift Connery high into the fading moonlight. But boldness leaves him when he feels anything real. And he does not tell her that he will be seeing Alex soon.

JOEY AND ANSLEY sit on a bench near Clubland's beach. Time is near noon.

Joey is not directly employed by Ansley. He is sort of assigned to him. He also accepts his bribes.

Joey is Deep State — who he works for changes with each conversation. CIA, NSA, ONI HHA BBA — who knows. When Joey is telling the truth he is usually lying. But he's a fit enough dude with Puerto Rican heritage and Marine sniper action. He's scary. But affable. He doesn't drink or do drugs. Instead he screws women at an incredibly high rate. They find his cockiness and wide smile charming. And he gives them just enough mystery to let them write the rest on their own. The best man for most women is the one they create. And Joey certainly oozes a particular masculinity that cries out dangerous fuck. That always helps too.

Joey has not shaved in a few days. His face doesn't grow stubble well so he looks appreciably wimpier. He's been bed hopping and none of the chicks had an unused razor.

Ansley is explaining the Connery situation to him. "So you see it could get tricky with Alex if I am dating Connery. So I might need your help with this."

"Get *tricky*? Fuck! What is that your idea of corporate-speak? Why don't you just use the money laundering stuff I gave you on Pacheco to calm him down? I mean it ain't much to get him nailed on dealing coke either."

"I don't want to Joe. I feel like that shit is a good gun to have. But you start waving a gun around and it loses its mystery. And it makes people too urgent and so their reaction can go nuclear."

"Alex wants to destroy you bud. He's trying to get you in on that dead senator's kid."

"Everyone knows that."

"Seems everyone but you! You're not even talking to me about fixing that shit. I thought that was why you wanted to meet. Instead you're talking about fucking with Alex's chick. The dude who wants you dead or in prison. You know he's hoping he can get you arrested and maybe that will discredit the blackmail you got on him. He doesn't give a fuck what you might leak on the other club owners. And who knows – maybe your dead man switch is shit. Or getting arrested will prevent you from flicking it. He hates you enough that he's taking chances bud. He hates you enough to not think clearly. Clubland is a jungle and the jungle leaders want you dead. That's a lot of bad hopes in your direction."

"Hear my plan out. I think it can work out in wondrous ways."

"You're thinking with your dick, asshole."

Ansley thinks, Actually I am thinking with my heart. My dick is too dumb to bother with this.

"Look hear me out Joe –"

"Ansley there's something bigger on this. Alex is a punk. And guys like him can cause damage but in the end they're not much. But somebody much higher –" Joey pauses for effect. "Somebody much much higher and behind the curtain has taken an interest in you and Clubland."

Ansley is disturbed that cool super-spy Joey seems spooked. "You got a name."

"The Man Behind the Curtain. And he doesn't care about your dead man switch. He doesn't care if all the people you got dirt on go down. You've got nothing on him and never could. And he can dig thru the background check I gave you. He knows the real you bud."

"The police –"

"Can't. They think you're the Ansley I made up. You'll survive them fine. But you won't survive The Man Behind the Curtain. And Alex Pacheco is an easy button for him to side with and push."

Ansley watches the waves, trying to think of options. "I know when we started this thing we said we're not friends. But I need a friend on this one. You in?"

Joey smiles. Rubs his silly stubble. "I may have some info that could help. It'll certainly surprise. Let's hear your plan. But remember bud: Everything has a cost."

ANSLEY LOVES to begin his Clubland nights at dusk. He stands at the open end of The Horseshoe facing the beach, watching the sky turn purple, then blue. Then he turns and starts the street walk.

Pat, who runs the sub shop Foot in Mouth, yells, "Ansley!" So does Rich who runs the Italian restaurant Mama Good. And Margaret, the crazy 80 year old who runs a balloon store. Which is surprisingly popular. And a pain in the ass. Balloons are floating all over the place and all it takes is a little gravity to turn a balloon into litter.

And on and on the hellos come. From the misfits he allows to run businesses, to leggy blondes, leggy brunettes, leggy redheads, leggy multi-colored hairs. Ex girlfriends and one night stands. Hangers on and the hopelessly dropped off. All say hello.

Ansley is wearing a grey suit made of silk and cotton, with Italian black loafers and cotton blue shirt. Everything on him is pricy. Classy. It's a funny thing because to see him in this environment you'd think he is obsessive about clothes. Actually he's more of a shorts/jeans guy. Ansley is kind of a slob. But for Clubland he becomes another character. Which is fitting because most of Ansley's worldview comes from watching way too many movies. And when he walks into Clubland he isolates little dramas playing out as if they're movies. He's a pretty good detective or stalker. His eyes at a distance usually perceive the juiciest gossip.

Stations is the best club in Clubland. Ansley has to give Alex that. It's a bright place, unlike the other clubs which worship darkness. It has light. It has levels. Has oddness and personality.

One floor is techno, one floor plays Van Halen, one floor is nothing but water bars and soothing blue lights and jazz. Alex has no taste but Julie, the chick who actually runs the joint, has a lot. Most of the club runners are content with creating large dark spaces full of sound. But Stations is something else. A place you can dance all night on ecstasy or have a beer to a Jimmy Buffet song. It's the only club that does a lot of day business.

Julie is a tall blonde. She recently cut her hair short. She looks better with long hair but she is the type of woman you'd never tell that to, even in jest.

Ansley is sure Alex and Julie fuck from time to time. But who doesn't in Clubland.

Ansley finds Julie on the ground floor. This is the old lobby area used for checkins when it was a hotel. It's been remodeled to act as a way station to get club goers to and fro. Hot chicks in tight tops and shorts sell shooters and instruct the newbies about the lays of the land.

Alex and Julie use the old front desk manager's office in back for important stuff. It's small and also locked 24/7. Only they have the three keys needed to get in. And plus Alex has it swept for bugs at least twice a month. The smallness of the office helps with that.

Ansley knows Alex and Julie feel safe in that office. Always hit them where they feel safe.

ANSLEY HAS to stand because there is only room in the office for two chairs. Alex's bodyguards – three thick brutes which could have come from central casting, keep a vigil outside.

Alex just turned 30. He has a mustache and thin body created by cocaine and lack of sleep. He is well dressed, silk shirt and Armani pants and tie. About six feet tall. Not a bad looking guy. But damn there is something about him that is so cheap it makes Ansley want to punch him every time he has to meet with him.

Alex would love to punch Ansley. "So why do we get a visit from our lord and savior?" he says.

Ansley smiles at Julie. "You guys saw me come into this office and stand right here." Pointing down at the floor, "Right here. Just right here. *Right*?"

"What the fuck is this about Ansley?" Alex demands.

"You saw I didn't go anywhere else but *this* space. Right where I am standing. Capiche?"

Alex keeps profanely demanding Ansley explain himself, but Julie is intrigued and keeps silent.

Ansley interrupts Alex's profane demands, "I am here to *help* you Alexander. I need your help with something and I am a gentleman and a scholar. So I don't come empty handed."

Ansley points toward the black curtain. "I know bugs are tough to kill. I think you exterminate a lot. I'd check that exterminator's license though."

Alex and Julie exchange glances and then he gets up and traces his hands from one side of the curtain to the other. When he finds the slickly placed bug his face drops.

"No telling how long a bug nest could be there if you've got an un-detailed exterminator," Ansley says.

Alex's anger crunches his face and he steps up on Ansley menacingly. "Out fucking side," he says.

∼

Nightlife is everywhere now on Clubland's car-less street. Music and footsteps are the dominant sounds as Alex, Ansley and Julie fight the great crowd for space.

"How the fuck did you know about that bug?" Alex demands as the madness of people pushes them closer. "I just had that place swept yesterday and he didn't find shit. So how the fuck? But I know how – you did it motherfucker! You planted that fucking shit!"

"You're under a serious FBI investigation Alex!" Ansley shouts. "Who do you use to sweep anyway?"

Alex stares him down. He has no intention of answering him.

Ansley feels bad about having to throw the sweeper guy under the bus. Alex will take his revenge. So he is having Joey scare the shit out of him first. Ansley sent an envelope with Joey that has enough cash to pay the sweeper dude's way out of town and then some. It does occur to Ansley though that no matter how much money you lay down, it doesn't excuse the dirty deeds that he engages in. And most of the time he does these lousy things without a second thought.

"Who watches the Watchmen, Alex. You put your faith in a tiny office with locks and a bug sweeper you really don't fucking know shit about. C'mon man – you done fucked up."

Julie is ready to chime in. "Ok so you knew about the bug and told us. But you didn't tell us without wanting something. Why are you here lord and savior?"

Ansley grins at Alex. "So Connery," he says.

Saying Connery's name pushes Alex's last button. He throws a punch at Ansley. But Ansley niftily avoids it and slips to his left to counter. Suddenly the street crowd has a show.

They circle each other and just before Alex can run at Ansley, Julie puts a stop to all of it by putting herself in harm's way. A few balloons fall in a timely fashion on the ruckus.

Ansley smirks theatrically to the crowd. It's obvious he loves being an asshole.

"Alexander. *Buddy*. Pal of mine. You know I have never done anything but love on you. And yet you try to cause me physical harm. I am your biggest fan Alexander. Whenever someone calls you the biggest asshole in Clubland, I defend you. I always tell them, No – there are way bigger assholes."

"Fucking cocksucker!"

"Always with the cock and sucking. Were you breast fed by the way?"

Alex is ready to lunge again but Julie stops him and then yells, "Fucking both of you stop!"

Alex can't stop. "Fucking with my woman is too far motherfucker!" He looks around at the crowd. "You all know he's a blackmailer motherfucker! He's a blackmailer asshole trying to screw my woman! And he'll try to fuck yours too because he's a *motherfucker* –"

Alex tries to kill Ansley again. But the bodyguards are outside by now and under Julie's orders they stop him this time. He's dragged inside. Loudly screaming insults which have motherfucker as every other word.

Julie walks over to Ansley. Grabbing him by the arm she leads him to the beach. Once there they sit on a bench watching the waves. The sound of Clubland is in back of them, both loud and yet distant.

"I know you like fucking with him," she says. "But this is dirty pool Ansley to go after Connery. Even for you."

"He follows the script of a hot headed latino so easily."

"What is it you want from us?" Her hazel eyes are cool. "No bullshit Ansley."

Ansley has long suspected that Julie is in love with Alex. She's a smart girl. Smart girls make the dumbest decisions in matters of romance.

"I am not trying to get with Connery."

"Right."

"Well I am not trying *much*."

"Go fuck yourself."

"I can't tell you how I know this but I think Connery is mixed up with that dead kid."

"Oh come on! She's a bartender! I don't think she ever met him. He got thrown out of Pink ages ago."

"I know Alex is close to this one Julie. He dealt blow to the kid.

Don't bother to deny it. It's a bad connection all around. It looks bad for Clubland if all this starts to shake out. Who poisoned this fucking kid anyway? Where did he get it? Why poison him anyway? Why not just overdose the fucker? My contacts have told me the supply chain of all this snakes back to Connery and me. Which is bullshit so someone is setting me up. I need Alex's help to make sure we both stay out of this."

Julie knows this is bullshit. She knows Ansley is aware that Alex is bribing the police and anyone else of relevance to tie him into the mess. She wonders now if it's better to act coy or call his bluff.

"Alex fucking hates you. So do I by the way."

"Irrelevant. I know Alex doesn't want Connery mixed in all this. Plus he's under a pretty severe FBI probe. One that got thru all your security and bugged you. God only knows what you two chitlins said in there. I have the FBI contacts that might be able to help him with this. That's why Alex should help me. He swims better if he does. And he might drown if he doesn't."

Julie looks into the ocean's darkness. "Stay away from him. And no dating Connery in Clubland. Especially his fucking club. I'll get back to you tomorrow. But so help me Ansley I know you're lying right now. Just know that I know." She stands. "Now fuck off from us for the rest of the night."

"You're a classy broad Julie," Ansley says. And then he heads toward Pink Lucid. Connery is on the bar tonight.

MIKE IS Pink's club manager. He also hates Ansley. He also has no choice but to tolerate his arrogance. Ansley is fond of ordering drinks for people and then telling Mike to just add it to his tab. Ansley has no tab of course. He does always tip the servers really well out of pocket. So they love Ansley.

"I need Connery on bar tonight," Mike says. "I don't have anyone to handle that section."

"Sure you do Mike. There are tons of girls who are trying to get a job in Clubland. Just make an announcement you're having a tryout and if your nipples are pointing east toward –"

"I don't have time for your bullshit –"

"I love magic. Love magicians. Remember that drug bust Mike – you were caught with coke and your dick in a 17 year old? A real magician made that one disappear. But you know overage dicks in 17 year olds. A good magician can make'em disappear and then reappear again with fresh charges. Now pay Connery what she would pull down for the night and get her the fuck out of here. Please and thank you."

Ansley would have respected Mike if he punched him. He would still work to destroy him but he'd have his respect. Instead Mike adjusts his glasses and tucks in his shirt – he is gaining weight and it is really starting to show.

Ansley touches his expanding belly with both hands. He says, "Blessed be the belly spread. It makes you more distinguished. To 17 year olds anyway."

Mike whispers insults as he walks away to pay Connery a lot of money not to bartend tonight.

∼

ON THE STREET of Clubland the crowd is moving now like a river going both ways. From above it might look as if Connery and Ansley are the only stationary objects.

"So Mike hates you too!" Connery says. She is wearing tight spandex clothes, turquoise top, black pants. Tropical bartender gear.

"Mike's such a *joiner*. He's a pathetic soulless pussy. You wanna drive my car?"

"You don't wanna drive?"

"No. No I don't." Ansley wants to think about her and not the road. He notices a red balloon floating above, almost as if it's seeking him out. Written on it in blue letters is: Beware the bricklayer you don't understand.

"What kind of car do you have?" Connery asks.

This is a question many have tried to answer. Since Clubland has no cars, seeing Ansley's ride is always off script from the nightlife. It's dark blue, small, sleek and foreign. It's familiar enough that the make almost slides off people's tongues. But they always stop short. They look for a metal plate branding but they find none. Top up or down doesn't help. And neither will Ansley. He relishes this mystery.

They drive thru tropical streets that have just been rained on and the night lights reflect off the dampness, making everything seem clean and new. The moon above is a big one and getting bigger. Beside him sits a girl who doesn't know how desperate things are. I know, he thinks, because me and you – we're the same. Ansley cannot see himself in a mirror. But in a nightclub's sweet sad bartender girl, he can't be missed.

Life suddenly seems open and possible as the cool breeze passes. Delicate lips and minds can become innocent again in hope. Love has no clock, he thinks, and it sure is a strange thing indeed.

∽

JOEY IS THANKING HIS OPERATIVE. How the hell the guy planted that bug today with Alex and Julie in the building – it was masterful. He hands him a large envelope. "I told you Ansley would pay," he says.

∽

AT SEASHELLS CONNERY drinks her first quickly. In the madness they start talking about her purse's contents.

"This is my makeup," she says, raising reverently a small circle of powder.

Ansley is shocked Connery wears makeup. Her face looks untouched by years or chemicals. "I never thought you wore makeup."

"I barely do. You see this stuff is natural and good for your skin. But I have *this* –" She raises another small circle of powder. "This is my backup. It's not as good as the first one I showed."

"But why isn't your backup of the good one?"

"Because they're changing it. They haven't yet but they're doing weird things man. And so I have this one as my backup because I might not be able to have that one soon."

"They haven't changed it yet though."

"No. But they're doing things. So I have this one as a backup."

"They're doing – or they have *done* them?"

"It's complicated!"

Smiling, "No it isn't. A girl's makeup, bra preference and wedding dress are three key ingredients to her secret sauce. And they all make you a little nuts."

Ansley is amused that even though Connery is without most female vanities, she still has a girl regimen of makeup. Unlike most chicks, she doesn't have a vanity table at home where tweezers pluck and powders powder over. She puts her makeup on in the car.

Ansley finds it sweet and affectionate that she trusts him to listen to her makeup ritual. She must know as a man he instinctively doesn't care about this shit. And yet she likes him enough to trust that'll he care now. It's a simple, kinda vulnerable gesture that touches him.

He asks, "Are you ever exhausted at being so popular?" Already the bar regulars have been coming over to say hello.

Connery's brown eyes lower. Her voice becomes huskier. "It's exhausting. I don't like it."

"And yet you never say fuck off."

Grinning, "Well that wouldn't be cool man!"

"Here's a thing I know that you think I don't know. It is not unnatural for you to be rude. Mean. To be *cutting*. You wanna know why you don't embrace that side more?"

"Why?"

"Because people have been that way to you and it hurt. So you give people the benefit of the doubt. You give everyone the benefit of the doubt. Especially drunks. You're popular because people sense that about you."

Connery takes a big sip. "I know something that maybe you don't think I know. I think you're *kind*. I think you don't like people knowing that shit. That's what I fucking think. Why don't you 'embrace' that?"

"I am not kind. I am a sociopath."

"Fucking bullshit. You are trying to help me. I am not sure with what but you are. And you haven't made a real pass at me. I usually would think you're a psycho but something else is going on in there."

"Maybe you just need help."

"I'm fine man."

"Then why stick around a guy with bandages if you're fine."

Connery opens her small mouth but only air comes out. Her lack of answer surprises her.

Ansley orders another round. We're gonna need a lot, he thinks.

DETECTIVE FRANK IS SITTING in Alex's small office. Julie has the other chair. Alex is leaning against a wall.

Detective Frank says, "Tell me what he said. But this time try to make it chronological." People's minds think in emotions and events. Cops only need a timeline.

Julie drinks a rare shot of whisky. She goes over the timeline of the night and then says, "He is trying to double bluff us on the senator's kid. He knows Alex is trying to link him to that poison business."

Detective Frank says, "He's a pretty clever guy this Ansley. He's not a sticky fellow. He comes in and out of our radar but always smoothly and never a scratch."

Alex kicks the wall he is leaning against. "That's *motherfucking* bullshit. Arrest him tonight! Who the fuck cares if anything *sticks*. It'll get him out of our way for a while."

Julie and Detective Frank exchange an uncomfortable glance.

Detective Frank addresses Alex but looks at Julie, "It isn't done this way. You don't own the DA. Or the judge who will hear the complaints filed by his lawyers. You don't get it Alex. Just because he's a sonuvabitch doesn't make him guilty. Even in a frame."

Alex kicks the wall again.

Julie says, "Frank can you lean on Ansley a little. Just as a breather. And find out if the FBI planted that bug or he did."

"I can look into the Feds. But I doubt I get far. I could just get a guy to follow you guys around and see if they see surveillance."

Julie is intrigued. "That's novel."

Detective Frank thinks a moment. "You guys do need to throw Ansley a curve ball. Shake him up. We need a chess move."

Julie looks at Alex. A wry smile forms. "Connery!" she yells.

"How many drinks have we had?" Ansley asks.

Connery thinks a moment. "Four."

"Four is an unlucky and unlikely number. Let's go for eleven."

"Do you mind if I smoke?"

"Yes." He smiles. "But you're gonna do it anyway. I didn't know you smoked."

"I don't everyday. It's more of a bar thing."

"You didn't smoke last time we were here."

"I didn't need to."

"I wonder what the hell that means."

Grinning, "I bet you do."

"Name your favorite movie."

"You know how many people ask me that in a bar? I don't have one."

"Color?"

"Don't have that one either."

"Car?"

Connery's eyes light up. "I love cars! I really liked yours by the way. I just didn't feel like talking on the way here. I really really love cars. But I can't think of a favorite."

"So you have no favorites. That makes you full of variety."

"I guess so. That's a cool way to look at it."

"There's always another way to look at it."

"Fuck you. Suck a dick! You always have more don't you."

Ansley says nothing.

Connery can't take his silence. "Ansley what do you have? You can't just stop on that."

"What do I have? Well you have nothing that you truly love. You don't have that one thing that really will break you apart if you can't love it, if it can't be only yours to connect with.

"You don't even have a favorite color or car. And you definitely don't have a favorite man either and never have. And the thing is darlin': You have a soul that needs to have a deep connection that is loyal and irreplaceable and if you don't find it, your life will be a failure. You can have all the faces in bars love you. And carry boyfriends around who don't ignite. Some people can live on variety like that. They can live on a bunch of crap everywhere in their lives. Not you. You are sparse baby. You need that one thing and you ain't got it and let's face it, you ain't looking for it. We all have something and that's yours."

Ansley signals the bartender for another round and then says, "Smoke up. There's more. Probably anyway."

JOEY IS TALKING to two private detectives. "Now you just need to give the *impression* you're FBI."

They both answer they can do that.

These guys are not good, he thinks, but Ansley said *not good* is even better.

DRINK NINE.

"I'm really fucked up," Ansley says. He hasn't been this lit in a long time.

"I am totally fucked up man," Connery says. She looks at Ansley, grinning. Studies his face a moment. "I really like your blue eyes."

Smiling, "A bit cliched. But I'll take it."

"I can't drive man. I'm fucked up."

"Like I can. We're gonna have to cab it." He goes over and pays the tab, asks the bartender to call a taxi.

The breeze is cool as they wait for the cab. They don't speak. They're going to his place but really both are wondering where they are going.

∽

ANSLEY'S PLACE is a renovated barn in the back of a large World War Two-era home. A white gazebo with a two seat swing sits to the side of it – Ansley often uses the swing when he feels stressed. The owners rarely visit and so the property is usually empty except for weekly upkeep servants.

Ansley loves the open space of the barn – the high ceiling and vastness release his mind, help him think.

It is sparsely furnished, with just a bed, a nightstand and bathroom at one end, a kitchen and dining table at the other and in the middle, a modern black lounge chair with ottoman, adjacent to a black cabinet which holds the stereo, vinyl and CD's; next to the chair is a table which usually holds Ansley's whiskey but is empty tonight. There's no television.

There is also a large and long black cabinet that holds Ansley's expensive, stylish clothes. It ends near the bed.

Ansley has placed lamps to strategically give off blue and strawberry lighting. He has a remote control for all his lights as well as his music and he flicks both on now. Some Isley Brothers seeps out into the vast space and Connery walks into a strawberry patch of light and smiles. She says, "No pictures on walls?"

"No pictures."

"I kinda thought you'd have beer lights or something."

"I give off the Schlitz Malt Liquor vibe huh."

"Fuck I don't know man. I just expected something. *More*."

Connery is at one end of the barn and Ansley is directly opposite her at the other end. When she takes a few steps, so does he and the tension between them builds.

Connery arrives at the lounge chair and picks up a few of the CD cases sitting around it. "You listen to a lot of different types of music," she says.

"Well life needs a soundtrack. You never know when a moment is gonna need Bach or David Lee Roth."

Connery places the CD's down on the table and absently walks again. Ansley follows her movement. When she stops, so does he. And the space between them intensifies.

"So how long have you lived here?" Connery says, but Ansley ignores her. He just smiles. Stays silent for a moment. Then, his blue eyes dead on her, he crosses the space separating them.

Connery actually takes a few steps back once he arrives, but Ansley raises his hand in a gentle gesture and she stops moving. They are close now, just lips and eyes.

Their first kiss is quick, and Connery pulls out of it for just a second – she needs to look into his eyes one last time before they go forward. Then Ansley engulfs Connery's small waist in his hands and lifts her to the whiskey table near the chair. Her legs wrap around him as his hands move upward – the first time you touch a woman with passion is always a wondrous sensation and Ansley moves his right hand lower. Connery flinches and pulls him tighter as his fingers press inside her and before she knows it they are in his bed, all the way entwined and no going back.

RANDY IS OFTEN EMBARRASSED at the comments Ansley makes. The gay sex scandal that ruined his career has made him scared to offend. As such, he has tried to make his everyday speech as PC as possible.

Even though Randy wishes to offend no one, he secretly hates everyone for making him this way and of course, feels guilty about that hate. He feels guilty about most things and really, almost nothing is ever the poor guy's fault.

Ansley enjoys making Randy feel inappropriate and so uses all the buzzwords he is not supposed to use. "How is the faggot trade in Clubland?" he asks. They are sitting at a cafe far away from The Horseshoe. It has good eggs and ok toast. The coffee is also just ok.

Randy has learned to ignore Ansley's fake bigotry. He hasn't learned to stop silently cursing him.

Ansley continues the torturing, "Yeah faggots. We are all faggots though right? In our own way. Faggots and kikes and whops and micks and niggas, that's just what we are – just a pile of human stew shit –"

"Ansley what is it you wanted to see me about?" I fucking really really hate him sometimes, he thinks. Randy is sure Ansley is the least sexist, homophobic and racist person he has ever met – he has a strange love of meritocracy combined with dividing the world into two camps: Asshole/Non-asshole. He only seems to care if you're good at something and you're not an asshole. Yet somehow his lack of bigotry makes his bigoted words even worse.

"You know Connery – that bartender at Pink?"

"You mean the one you're dating to piss Alex off."

"That's not entirely true."

"Oh yes it is 'entirely' true. You're a prick. But I wanted to see you about this senator's kid thing. Me and Jen have been taking the pulse of The Horseshoe and it's kinda scary for you. There are whispers everywhere."

"I've spoken to the police twice."

"Well I have a contact there too." This means Randy met a cop who likes hanging in Clubland and he has arranged quite a few VIP nights for him. It also might mean the cop in question is gay and Randy is getting some. Ansley hopes that's true.

"I think they put a tail on you Ansley."

Ansley picks at his over-easy eggs. He tastes a strip of bacon. He can't help but find all of this amusing. He has hired two private detectives to trail Alex and Julie as if they're FBI, even though he knows Julie will see thru that ruse immediately. The cops are trailing Ansley because Alex has managed a breakthrough bribe to counteract

Ansley's usual police bribes. And Joey is also stalking Alex because Ansley asked him to, and probably stalking Ansley because of his own spook reasons. And some of the other club runners, while wishing Ansley great harm, are very nervous he'll use his dead man switch if he gets caught up in this murder nonsense. So they also have people, informal and not so informal, all over Clubland scoping things out. You need a cross in order to double cross and who the hell knows where anybody is standing right now.

And also there is a special tail on Ansley – and he had sensed this before Joey told him about someone high up taking an interest in him; now he's sure this tail, which is usually done by a knockout girl, is from this unknown Man Behind the Curtain. It isn't unusual for Ansley to be followed. Since day one plenty of the club leasers have hired all kinds of gumshoes to figure him out. But there is something different about the tails this Mr. Big has initiated. If anything, they are harder to spot and when spotted, they never panic. And Ansley isn't sure if being spotted is part of the plan.

"We are all being followed right now," Ansley says. "24/7. From somebody by everybody. Listen. I am in the middle of a plan. It's a little dangerous. But mostly weird." He grins. "It's so *me* Randy. So let me fill you in. I don't want you or Jen hurt by it. But I need both of you in it."

"Ok," Randy says and listens intently. When Ansley is done explaining the plan, he takes a big sip of OJ. "That plan is nuts! It makes no sense. It goes on and on and all you need is a few moves. And oh yeah you barely know this Connery girl! Why are you risking the world for her!"

"Mirrors are strange things," Ansley says.

"What the fuck does that mean? You must think you're in love. You fell in love with some bartender that just happens to be Alex's girlfriend. Oh fuck it!"

"I am not in love."

"Oh that helps. Do all this crazy shit for a chick you don't love. And maybe you aren't. Maybe you just wanna piss Alex off more than usual."

"You keep saying Alex. All the club dudes despise me. He's not special."

"I think he is special Ansley. Because he's the only one whose girlfriend you're fucking."

"Are you gonna help me Randy?"

"Jen isn't going to like this."

"That's not my question."

Randy has had enough of his meal. "Listen you've caused a lot of shit in just a few years. And I'm grateful for you helping me. But I need to tell you something that's been really bothering me."

"Well tell me."

"I think you're insane. And not in a oh-he-be-so-crazy-but-cool-kinda way. I think you're legitimately mental. You need help. You have shop people and restaurant people – and I grant you they're fun people – but they're nuts and you just spend whatever money of your own to set them up. And the wackier – the more money you throw at them. It's like you're only interested in saving the world for fucked up people. And you'll burn everyone else's world down to do it."

Ansley has never heard Randy be this honest with him sober. "Do you consider yourself fucked up?"

"I hate myself. But it's really condescending to me when you think you have to 'save' me. I wanna live my life motherfucker. I don't walk around wondering if you can save me. And if I can only be saved by a crazy man like you, then I am kinda fucked aren't I?"

Randy decides to order another coffee. He drinks it in one gulp. "And another thing," he says. "What about this girl Connery? You're risking everything for her and ok I think that's nuts. But you wanna know what's really nuts? Love her or not, you and I both know you have no intention of keeping her around."

Ansley sips his coffee. It's too hot. "Yes I do."

"No you don't. You never keep any girl around." Randy orders another coffee. "This isn't going to end well," he says.

∽

RANDY SITS in a Denny's diner. He thinks only of Ansley's insanity. And he's going nuttier by the second.

The other day he gave a shop to a woman who wants to knit you socks while you wait. He allowed another lady to open up a portrait shop. What kind of portraits? You bring in your high school yearbook photo and she'll paint it for you. She's very strict, though. It *has* to be a high school yearbook photo. And no blondes, please.

All over, Clubland has these freaks. In Ansley's smirk Randy detects revenge. It's like he's sticking it to the world for sticking it to him. Except Ansley has never told anyone why he hates the world and at 24, he hasn't lived enough for people to just assume he'd be bitter. There's also a self-destructive streak running thru Ansley that Randy fears will take them both down.

When Ansley hired Randy, he never told him his hobby is blackmailing people. Arson, art forgery, murder, tax evasion, sex kinks, money laundering – he's got shit on everybody. It's a never ending list compiled it seems by his shadowy buddy Joey, who Randy figured out right away is Deep State.

And Randy, being a former DC guy, has noticed the increasing place that politics is finding in Clubland. He sees the guys and gals who influence the political decision makers dealing and fondling all night, every night, in Clubland. A few exits down the highway the capital governs, but so many of its policies are decided in the flash and dash of The Horseshoe. Rock stars and movie stars are common now. This has grown into something beyond the physical. Clubland is an idea now as much as a place. And Randy is worried that the idea is in the head of a crazy man.

Jen joins him, slips into the booth. She is beautiful, tired, and pissed off.

"So why did you want me here this early?" 3pm to her is 4am to most.

"Ansley is crazy," he says.

"Fucking tell me something I don't know." Jen, being bipolar, is also crazy, but in a more textbook way than Ansley. She refuses to treat her bipolar disorder because of the drugs' side affects. She also knows this isn't tenable.

"He's always been crazy," she says. "So what's different today?"

"He is running a fake FBI investigation on Alex."

Jen laughs. She doesn't even ask why. "What else?"

"He intends to frame himself for the murder of that senator's kid."

"What!" She fumbles for words. "But why? Why? But why?"

"Oh it gets better," Randy says.

∽

Ansley is driving to Clubland. He spots in his rearview a new tail. The guy is unkept in a wrinkled cheap grey suit and white beard. Not a cop. Probably a cheap PI sent by one of the club runners.

Ansley decides to have a little fun. He takes a detour down a narrow two lane road. He doesn't hit the gas hard right away. He eases his speed up slowly. But eventually he's going 90 and weaving. His tail is in an old Toyota and not as good a driver as Ansley. He can't keep up. So Ansley slows down.

Once the tail catches up Ansley leads him down an even narrower road. He flips into high gear and suddenly he's hitting near a hundred again. The old Toyota behind him does its feeble best to keep up.

And the road keeps getting narrower and narrower.

Unbeknownst to the tail is that this road ends at a pond. And the closer you get to the pond, the darker the road. If you don't know it's there, you won't know it's there.

Ansley blasts toward the pond now and then at the last second, shifts down and does a crazy turn. He misses the pond by inches.

The Toyota has no such luck. It hits the pond full force. The poor unkept bastard in it stumbles out, haggard and dazed.

Ansley pulls alongside him and says, "Be careful of gravity and dirty water. They cause impotence."

∽

ANSLEY DOES ENJOY his grand entrances in Clubland. He wears a striking pink suit tonight with black shoes and white silk shirt. He walks thru Clubland's car-less street feeling alive, the wind in his hair, a grin graced by two-day stubble and cocky indifference. He glides thru kitchens saying hello to the staff, he chats up every DJ, flirts with and slyly admires the short skirts. His eyes are on every little drama, filing away who is fighting with whom and who broke whose heart. It's all here in Clubland. Desperation, desire, love, drugs, sacrifice, delusion, even redemption. One silly stretch of land playing loud music and slinging pricy drinks somehow has the entire contents of the human soul on display.

Ansley spots Joey in the corner of Club Siphon. They get a VIP booth. Neither drink.

Joey says, "So I hired the weird bad private detectives you asked for."

"I know. They're wonderfully obvious. I saw them poking around. And I know Julie did! Have you pushed the timeline so this gets over soon?"

"Yes. But this is a big big favor bud. Remember the costs will come due."

Ansley knows he is going to have to participate in something that will compromise his soul. Still he presses on. "How lucky are we anyway? As bad as you thought?"

"Even worse. No one is without dirt. And this guy – fuck he needs a shovel."

Ansley smiles. No decent man can be found in all of Sodom.

∽

JEN AND RANDY sit in a Mexican restaurant far away from Clubland. Detective Frank sits on the opposite side of the booth drinking coffee. He is suspicious of their story. He's been busy trying to frame Ansley for the murder of the senator's kid. And here they are claiming that not only did he do it, but they have a taped confession.

"Why would he kill the kid?" Detective Frank demands. "I need a motive."

Randy looks at Jen, who gives him a look that says: You say Ansley's shit, not me.

"The kid's dad is Senator Wiley. He's the chairman of some arms committee. A lot of the backing for The Horseshoe comes from para military companies and arms manufacturers."

"Why would these companies back something like Clubland?"

"Geez. You haven't seen how much political shit goes thru Clubland? How people find themselves compromised there? And hell these companies main offices are in our state. They want our state policies and our Washington reps aligned. And this Wiley wasn't aligned. These guys want him off that big committee or scared. And this Senator Wiley does have two more sons he'd like to live."

"So the arms business risks giving a murder job to someone like Ansley? C'mon."

"None of the money they have in Clubland is traceable," Randy says. "And Ansley – they own him with that untraceable money. They had nothing to lose giving him the job. If he fucks it up, so what? He goes down for life and they step in and take all of Clubland. This kind of power lives in the clouds.

"Ansley popped the kid with a poison. It looked like an overdose but with a senator's kid they look *very* closely. And give Ansley credit: You can't trace a poison like you can a gun. Especially the one he used. He turned out to be a good choice. These fuckers have a knack at spotting darkness in people. And the senator got the message. Believe me."

Detective Frank thinks about the poison. He tries to remember the name of it but it's unpronounceable. It's easy to make too. Mostly stuff you buy at the supermarket mixed with some weird ingredient – the weird ingredient is the worst kind – exotic but not something sold on black markets.

"Who would even believe Ansley if he tried to flip on the arms guys?" Jen adds. She smiles because she knows men love her smile. "There's no paper trail. It's just too insane of a story."

Randy jumps back in, "They'd find a way to mix up Ansley into some drug trade if he tried to flip on them. Smear him as a kiddie porn guy – beats puppies, drowns babies. They'd unleash all The Apparatus against him. No, Ansley was perfect because he is owned. And the message got thru to the senator: As long as he goes along with their war plan preparations, his other kids will live and his dead kid can become a martyr for the noble Drug War."

Detective Frank sips his coffee. He was going to get burritos but not now. His stomach is in knots because of his thoughts. "I want that goddamn tape today. And why did you guys decide to turn on him and make it?"

Randy and Jen look at each other. They begin to laugh.

"Because Ansley's crazy!" they both say.

"And we want away from him," Randy says. "We want Clubland. We wanna sell his share to the arms guys and cash out."

"He left his fifty percent to us," Jen says. "We have copies of his will. If he dies we get it. If he becomes incapacitated, we get it. Prison is listed in the incapacitation."

Detective Frank shakes his head. "He left The Horseshoe to you two?"

"Yes," Randy says. "He's fucking crazy!"

～

FEELING high from the good news from Joey, Ansley strides some more thru his Kingdom. Waitresses hug him and he playfully slaps some asses here and there. Some chicks kiss him – which doesn't seem impulsive when the pulsating music is blaring. Things are good and he feels great as he takes in the rush and loudness of his creation.

Then he hits Club Scion. Randy and Jen are waiting for him.

"Did you and Jen get done what I asked?"

Randy's face is serious. "Yeah. But you need to know something. We just found out."

Ansley checks Jen's face. It is as serious as Randy's.

Randy says, "Connery is in the hospital."

∼

Alex ruled out Julie's Big Idea involving Connery as a distraction for Ansley. So Julie went around him and hired a brute.

He forced his way into Connery's small place with a slap. Then he delivered Julie's words verbatim, "You wanna fuck around like a whore on Alex Pacheco. This is what happens to whore bitches."

Also per Julie's instructions, he made sure to deliver one solid knockout punch.

∼

Connery's button nose looks even more pushed in. Her right eye is closed and surrounded by black.

Ansley wants to throw up.

He reaches for her hand. "I didn't...."

I am responsible for this, he thinks. This is my fault. He wonders if he is trying to do good in the world or if he is crazy and dangerous.

Connery cries for a bit. But Ansley is amazed that she also makes a few jokes. "I guess Alex and I are really broken up now," she says.

"He's a sonuvabitch," Ansley says and Connery, thru her one open eye, can see that he is thinking of the best way to kill Alex.

"Don't Ansley. I just wanna...get out of here. Go someplace else." Her one open eye looks at him with disappointment. She knows this is my fault, he thinks. She knows I put the spotlight on her.

Ansley stumbles for words for a while but Connery doesn't hear most of them. Finally a nurse ushers him away.

A coldness overtakes Ansley as he walks out of the hospital. A coldness that makes him calm where he should be reckless. He parses out all the steps in this. And he knows this doesn't add up. If Alex were a chick beater, he'd have done it by now. He uses uppers to flex his macho, he's an asshole, he's a cheater...but never has he hit any chick in Clubland or sent someone to beat on a chick. An impulsive asshole like him would have done both by now if it were in his nature.

Ansley sits in his stylish car for a while thinking. It wasn't Alex who gave the order. That leaves only one person with motive and opportunity.

∼

Alex Pacheco is leaving the apartment of a one night stand. He is smiling because the girl gave him a lot to smile about. It is 5am. He has not been in Clubland tonight. He has no idea about Connery.

It is unfortunate for Alex that his car is parked in a remote space. Not a lot of action here. No one to witness or help.

When Alex reaches his car, Ansley flies out of nowhere and hits his back with a baseball bat.

Standing over Alex, Ansley spits on him. "You have fun with your coke whore?"

He then puts on brass knuckles and gives Alex a beating that will take months to recover from. Alex coughs blood, screams out whys, even begs for mercy. He's just a hair's breath from death when Ansley stops.

Looking at Alex's writhing body, Ansley vomits and then vomits some more. He abhors violence and always has. As an orphan in some foster homes he was on the receiving end plenty. His conscience is not cut out for this. He is learning an important thing: What you are capable of and what you can live with are not the same thing.

∼

Ansley drives to the nearest gas station with a phone booth. He gets out, puts in the quarter and waits for an answer.

"Hello?"

"It's done."

Ansley hangs up. And then all his nerves collapse. His body convulses and he falls to the ground. He sees only violence. Connery's damaged pretty face and then the beating he has given to

Alex. The blood, bruises and life he just took from another human being, for Alex will be in a hospital bed for a while.

I really am not better than any of them, he thinks. I'm an immoral piece of shit too.

∼

DETECTIVE FRANK IS SUFFICIENTLY IMPRESSED with the confession tape that he arrests Ansley at 9am sharp as he is walking out of a Denny's diner. He makes a show of it – Detective Frank has press everywhere to immortalize the moment.

Ansley's face is down, his eyes full of shame. He looks as if he's being walked to the guilotine.

The morning reporters love it all and blast Ansley's shame all over.

Detective Frank cuts out early and goes to a local bar to celebrate. He buys a few rounds. On the bar's old TV, the morning news has him a hero.

And then Joey makes a phone call. "Better for it to be today," he says. "Not tomorrow. Take him today instead."

The evening news goes like this: "Cop frames local business owner for murder. FBI have been investigating a child pornography and trafficking ring in our community. Police have confiscated many items from Detective Frank Baraucha's home. Detective Baraucha's motives for framing Ansley Parade, owner of the popular Clubland, are still not known but are suspected to be related to the detective's drug dealing.

"Detective Baraucha's wife has declined comment. She has asked that the press respect her privacy right now for the sake of her two children. And now we go to the Police Chief for his word on the scandal."

∼

WHEN THE DUST settled it was a good story.

The FBI found kiddie porn all over Detective Frank's home office. It never occurred to Detective Frank how traceable the Internet is. He isn't an idiot but he isn't tech savvy either and the Internet is so new in 1994, most new users of it think of it as magical, not HTML code. Radio, movies, television – all new technologies seem magical to the first laymen users of it. Things like IP addresses and server logs, only the biggest of nerds know about crap like that in 1994. And the kiddie porn pics were so easy to get – his forbidden needs just couldn't resist. Once the jurors saw his computer files, the guilty verdict was in the bag.

The FBI had been onto him for a while. He was a key cog in a ring of perverts they would take down. Ansley had no idea about any of this until Joey told him. And upon hearing it, Ansley finalized his crackpot "fun" gambit.

Ansley wanted fake FBI guys to follow Alex and Julie just to screw with them. It was all just silly noise.

And Joey personally planted drug dealer evidence in Detective Frank's garage that showed the senator's coked-up kid owed him a lot of cash – it's easy to make a pedophile into a drug trafficker. The connection wasn't enough for a formal murder charge, but definitely enough for the court of public opinion to convict.

The cops and the press bought the story with no edits needed: Detective Frank killed the senator's kid over drug money owed. And he wanted to expand his drug business in Clubland, but he knew Ansley was incorruptible and would move against him once his drug traffic got too big to miss. So Frank decided to frame Ansley for the murder he committed. As a bonus Ansley was high profile and those are always career-boosting collars.

The city fathers ran for cover because this was one fucked up scandal. Cop selling drugs, collecting kiddie porn and killing a senator's son over a drug debt! Framing a local businessman. They would be busy for a while on the cleanup job.

Of course Ansley used the scandal to get brownie points with the Mayor, Police Chief – any and all he could have embarrassed and sued.

As for the confession tape, well. It disappeared. Detective Frank had played it over the phone for the DA before moving against Ansley. There was a minor internal investigation trying to find out what happened to it. But neither the DA or the police bureaucracy wanted to defend a pedophile and also, drag this scandal out any longer than it needed to be. So the investigation quietly was filed away in that place that no one looks unless you know where to look. The DA eventually gave a written statement that it must have been a fake.

Randy and Jen breathed a sigh when the whole mountain finally fell. Ansley had warned them that if anything went wrong it might get hairy. Luckily nothing went wrong, but the original goal of his crazy gambit fell short. Alex was supposed to get mixed up in the drug part of this and be sent away for a few years, thus taking him out of Connery's life. True Ansley Fuck You Theater.

But then Alex got an ass beating from Ansley which took him out of the drama. But that was the deal Ansley made.

∼

Ansley sits on a bench. In front of him is beach and ocean. It is morning and there is only a slight breeze and so the waves are calm.

Julie says, "We're done Ansley. I know I'm glad."

Ansley has to ask, "I know you love Alex. So why did you demand I beat him senseless?"

"You were going to anyway."

"Not when I figured out it was you."

"So then why didn't you put me in a hospital bed?"

Their eyes meet uncomfortably. It is a good question. Violence against men is repugnant to Ansley but violence against a woman is unforgivable. He hopes. He feels a quick sting of the rage he had when he saw Connery's damaged face and wants to punch Julie now.

When he confronted Julie on the night it all went down, busting into her house and ready to smash her face in, she started to cry. Since Ansley has a savior complex when it comes to women, the tears bought her some time. And then she started to make him offers to fix the situation – and for some reason, Ansley screamed all he wanted out of this was for Connery to end up on a farm, and Julie's crying eyes lit up....

And now Ansley studies Julie's hazel eyes – there is a grayness to them today. They're inscrutable. Calculating. In a flash he sees a resentment that must have roots in childhood. That resentment got aimed at Alex – you often resent the thing you love. Connery was just collateral damage and female sexual jealousy run amok. Staring into her eyes, Ansley becomes convinced that Julie needs to be the one to damage Alex and then nurse him back.

"You could have gone thru with your plan even if you figured out it was me," Julie says. "The frame would have gotten Alex out of the way – that's what you were going to do to him right? Mix him up in Frank's demise. You could have done that and kept me thinking my plan was working. You would have had a play against me if you needed it. Why didn't you?"

"When I figured out it was you who hurt Connery, I wanted to kill you. I wasn't thinking about Alex. When I calmed down I realized I needed to know your endgame in all this. And I figured that out."

"What is it then?"

Ansley smiles. "Love." He goes silent a moment, then, "Do you have enough to convince Alex that Detective Frank manipulated me into doing it as part of the frame up? I look like a drug dealer fighting with my supplier. Blah blah. And then Frank takes me out and makes a play at – I don't know – Clubland? Do you have a story he'll buy? Because I gotta tell ya, I ain't buying any of this. None of it balances right."

Fair questions but Julie has been at Alex's side every chance she can. There's a softening in his eyes. She is seeing the leaving of the criminal and the beginning of somebody else.

"It'll work out," she says. "I am selling our lease on the club. And you will allow it."

"Of course. And the deed to your small wonderful family farm?"

Julie reaches in her purse for the paperwork. "It's all arranged."

"I'll have attorneys check this," Ansley says. "They're best at making sure hearts are pure."

Julie smiles. She has to tell him, "I didn't think you'd figure out I did it. I thought your rage would focus only on Alex and blind you to everything. I told the brute to not hurt Connery too much. I did have a plan to fuck you and it was good too. You were smart to come to me. You would have been fucked if you tried to frame Alex. I would have gotten you. I had a good plan. But it relied on you not figuring it was me."

She gives him a look that says she respects him. Ansley finds her repugnant.

"You're a cunt," he says. "And this farm better be what you say it is."

"Even with your money you wouldn't find a better one. And you needed a quick one didn't you – you fucking piece of *shit* blackmailer."

Julie sees the farm in her mind's eye and it brings up childhood traumas. She becomes disgusted. "Your princess will find herself nicely there."

"Why do you hate this farm if it's so great? Bad childhood shit? You got beat or molested or maybe you just didn't get loved because you're a cold bitch. And a cold bitch can never understand love."

"Fuck you Ansley," Julie says and rises.

Ansley stares at the waves. "You ever hurt Connery again and your tits and pussy won't stop me."

Grinning, "Big words. Small men need them I guess."

In a month, a rehabilitating Alex and she will fly to an island far away from Clubland. The club lease sale brought a lot of money, but they wouldn't have needed it. Julie is wealthy – Alex never knew this. He still does not know. He will never know a lot of things about the woman who loves him.

∼

THE LAST MATTER was to say goodbye to Connery.

Ansley presented the small farm to her with pictures Julie gave him. And also lies about how he got it. But it was hers. She owned it. The taxes paid up for five years. It will be her space to find herself.

Ansley sees life as humans clawing and crawling for space. Physical space and mental space – trying always to find something that gives both of those and lets us be human without having to try so hard. The universe, in the form of Ansley, has done this for Connery. At least that's what he hopes. And the whole drama has broken Alex and his ilk from ever turning her heart back into stasis. It'll move toward something better.

Or so Ansley hopes.

Their last night together was spent in his barn. Connery's face had healed – her button nose was actually cuter now – and Ansley took a moment to freeze frame her gentle eyes and mischievous grin. Connery liked to call people "good humans" and she was one of the best he'd ever met. Ansley had fallen in love with her – if he wasn't sure of that before, he was sure now. He thought he'd just like her a lot and let her go. But this was different. This was love and letting that go was, in a way, suicide.

He didn't try to sleep with her. But he did hold Connery for a long, long time and when he kissed her goodbye it was filled with love. But it was also sad and defeated. And that kiss made Connery cry all the way to her new life.

∼

SOMETHING RANDY SAID after Connery was gone will not let Ansley sleep:

"I think you played a game that only you would want to play. God knows why. And you won a lot. I admit it. Won political points. Got the police off your back for the senator's kid. Scared everybody silly and increased your legend. And fucked Alex over. But I don't think you won anything for Connery. I think you did some emotional math and figured she's better off on a farm without you. I can't even believe I just said that sentence. Geez that sounds nuts!

"But life isn't about math Ansley. The best stuff is the *gut*. Do you ever think that God intended you guys to be with each other? And she might get lost all over again without you? That letting her go makes you a coward and a failure? Do you ever fucking think that maybe you needed that farm too?"

∼

JOEY SITS in a large dark office. It's a cliché for men of power but it's one they enjoy.

Ansley has no idea about this meeting. This is the part of Joey that Ansley has no privileged insight. The public blamed Detective Frank for the senator's kid – but that was bullshit. Who did kill him?

Ansley is sure it's The Man Behind the Curtain. And that is who sits before Joey now.

He says, "I never could conceive of the plan he came up with. It was fun to watch. I'll give him that. Like a movie. But I don't think he realizes what insight it gives into him. It changes our next move. Ansley is a man who thinks he's in a movie. And I think he'll be surprised at the movie we're gonna make."

3

APRIL 7TH, 1994

Since Connery's departure Ansley has picked up smoking. He doesn't need more bad habits and yet here he is at 3am, lying in bed and blowing smoke toward the ceiling. His barn is slightly lit in strawberry and blue.

Amanda is here. She is wearing her blonde hair up tight, her black skirt is both business-professional and tight. Her blouse is white and tight as well. Her pink rimmed glasses are pure geek and her red heels are higher than a normal librarian's would be – and that's what she is pretending to be: A librarian. It's Thursday – that's librarian night.

Ansley smokes and thinks. He wonders if Connery is happy. He wonders if he should have said I love you and not let her go. He thinks, Maybe Randy is right. Maybe I really did fuck up, even if I was trying to do the right good thing....

He should have been thinking about all the strange things lately that have been happening in Clubland. At least thinking about Rikon, the club runner of Brass Rings, who arrived last week to find his club destroyed on the inside. The detectives investigating are sure that whoever did it both had specific items they were looking for and yet also wanted to be destructive. And boy were they destructive – the club hasn't reopened since.

Out of all the club runners, Rikon is the only honest one. Ansley was doing business in a local hotel bar when he met him. He and his wife were on vacation. He had come into some inheritance and wanted to relocate from cold Ohio. And like most of Ansley's life decisions and friends, bar drinks were involved. They bonded. And he offered Rikon a club space for virtually nothing. Sadly they hadn't remained close friends because once Rikon started running his club, he saw the blackmails and other dirty deeds that Ansley does on a daily basis, often with glee. He became afraid of him. And the fear in his eyes act like a bad mirror to Ansley.

Smiling, Amanda leans over Ansley's smoke rings now. He is always amazed at how sexy she is – she earns the word stunning.

"Ansley it is Thursday and *you're* the one who wanted librarian."

"I know. And you look great by the way."

"You haven't looked at me Ansley! You've been staring at the ceiling."

Amanda takes the cigarette from his fingers and puts it out. She then takes her glasses off. They're just props – her vision is perfect. "What should I read from?"

Ansley smiles. "Tender is The Night. Book one. Chapter two."

Amanda goes to her purse and fiddles with a few books. Out comes Fitzgerald and she returns, slipping off her tight skirt and easing a button or two on her blouse. She slowly climbs into his bed, slithering here and there until she is straddling him. "We thought maybe you were in the plot," she begins.

Ansley's smile gets bigger. He grows harder as Amanda beautifully enunciates Fitzgerald's prose, easing more and more blouse buttons with each page until his hands are removing her bra and she drops the book. All of her comes to him as he starts to kiss her neck and breasts. Amanda is a wonderful fuck buddy and has helped him with mourning Connery's leaving. And he feels guilty because she is wonderful enough that another woman should never enter his mind in the throes of passion. But one has.

Ansley has not been able to stop thinking about this new woman, nor escape her presence. The Man Behind the Curtain has settled on her as his main tail. It unnerves Ansley that out of all the beautiful women he's sent to tail him in the past two months, he knew the one whose smile Ansley has fallen for. A little investigation of waiters revealed her name: Siema.

Ansley thinks of her name as he ravishes Amanda's tight body. He thinks of her smile and olive skin and dark hair and blue eyes – which are even more striking than his. All of her is an Arabic beauty, except for those eyes; he's sure some part of her is Irish. She must come from a mixed marriage, a split upbringing, Christian and Muslim, anglicized and Arabic. He wonders, What is it about those eyes that make me think of a sly pop song? Something strong and sly about Siema. Search as he might he can't find the rhymes to match her.

As he enters Amanda, Ansley is seeing Siema. Am I right about her past? It will turn out yes, he is. But the rest is going to be one hell of a surprise.

4

BLUE EYES AND SAD LYRICS AREN'T ENOUGH

It's an event night at The Horseshoe. Ansley has arranged fireworks to start at 11:30pm. That's still a few hours away and he is walking thru the crowd, surveilling. Across the way he sees Margaret, 80 years old but looking a 100. Her back is hunched and her face consists of wrinkles and two brown eyes. She still can move fast though and she's waving him into her balloon store.

Ansley is always weirded out by Margaret's balloon store. It feels like a funeral home made of glass. Every few steps there are balloons, glass counters and air pumps.

Margaret's cigarette stained voice wastes no time. "What the fuck is going on Ansley with you?"

"Margaret with a voice like that I don't know how the world of show tunes let you get away."

"They fucked up Rikon's place. All the shop owners know we're next."

"Rikon is going to be fine."

"Fuck you with your *fine*! You walk around in these expensive suits – you look like a faggot tonight by the way in this blue one."

"If faggot means I'm impossibly attractive to straight women – you got me honey."

"No it means you're a faggot gay. And I'm not going down without a fight."

Margaret's hunched self moves fast into the back and reemerges with a shotgun. She holds it out toward Ansley. "See I will kill the fuckers."

Ansley stares at the shotgun and then Margaret, thinking: Jesus Christ – if this is her at 80 – how many bodies were there when she was 20?

"Margaret this is overboard without a paddle. Put the fucking shotgun away."

"No fucking way dickhead." She cradles it while she lights a cig. "I'm not going to let some cocksuckers ransack my place the way they got Rikon's. I don't know what you're into. But what happened there was a message to you."

"Why is it always about me Margaret? Why is everything about fucking me!"

"Because you're a jackass!"

Ansley grabs the shotgun out of Margaret's hands. She's shocked he's so fast. Holding the shotgun high and away, "Look you crazy old bag! There's no reason for you to sleep in this weird fucking store of yours day and night with this goddamn shotgun waiting to shoot people!"

"You fucked up Ansley!"

"Jesus Lord have mercy." He hands her the shotgun. "Don't kill anybody tonight Margaret. Just give me a chance to sort this out."

Margaret puts the shotgun down and goes behind a glass counter. She pulls out a balloon and fills it full of air, handing it to Ansley. It says in blue and red lettering: Time Tricks For All.

"Thanks for this Margaret. I'll treasure it."

Outside Ansley gladly lets the weird balloon float away. Yet the wind patterns keep it above him. He can't shake it. He knows Siema is behind him. He doesn't want to shake her, in fact he'd like to formally meet her tonight. But he's got business at Pink Lucid.

∽

Seeing Margaret crazy, Ansley imagines his other wackos in similar straights. They're sad people who can only function in Ansley's Clubland. And the real world is trying to knock that down.

Pink Lucid's leaser is Charlie Flight. He's waiting for Ansley as he enters. A thin, tall man nearing 60, he looks older. A questionable life will do that to you.

They walk thru the madness of the club. Everywhere hot chicks twirl and grind. In the lights and beats of the DJ beautiful coked up women burn desperation. Champagne pops. And everywhere egos and glasses are filled past their limits.

It takes awhile to reach Charlie's office. He isn't happy. They both stand even though chairs are near.

"I've met with the other leasers," Charlie starts. "And they aren't going to stand for what happened to Rikon."

Ansley is annoyed. One good ransacking has the whole damn thing going to pieces. "Charlie it's one night of vandalism."

"We blame you!"

"Why the fuck does everyone blame me!"

"Because you're an asshole Ansley. And we have too much invested to lose it all. And if we're gonna lose everything anyway, well – fuck your blackmail."

Charlie's black eyes look like death incarnate to Ansley. "We're going to take you with us, Ansley," he says.

"Geez you people are skittish! I got this. You guys are out of your fucking minds."

Charlie takes a step toward Ansley. He has several inches on him and although he's thin and old, he's also lead a mean life and every part of his stare conveys this.

"How do you 'got this'? Whoever did Rikon's place has the police backing off enough to both not look bad and yet not get anywhere. Rikon's was just the start. What are you doing to end it there?"

Ansley takes a seat. "Charlie what is it you want from me?"

Charlie does not take a seat. "A plan."

Ansley stares into nothingness for a moment. And then he raises his head toward tall Charlie. He thinks of something crazy and then says, "Ok. How does this one sound...."

∼

THE FIREWORKS ARE GOING off now and the crowd is swaying to an imaginary song as the sky colors up in reds and blues and yellows.

Ansley is tired. Behind him is Siema. She follows tonight dressed in all black. He almost turns around to talk to her for the first time. But he can't bring himself to do it. He just walks toward the beach. Siema follows.

In this line of work Siema is relatively new, but her military experience prepared her for a lot. But not for Ansley. She was handed a dossier but this guy is not a dossier. She watches him collapse onto the beach sand. He holds his head in a sad way – it's clear he wishes for soft female hands to comfort him. But Ansley is an orphan. Alone. A man in an expensive suit sitting in sand, staring at a darkness which hides the ocean while his creation is alight and alive behind him.

He can't see the ocean and he can't look at his creation. Siema realizes that Ansley is both a man without a country and a man choked with responsibility. And when he holds his head again, Siema thinks of him as a little boy who never found a home to hold him.

∼

ANOTHER DAY HAS PASSED and nothing is solved. Ansley walks thru Brass Rings still amazed at the damage. They smashed and burned and took out key electrical infrastructure. Whoever did this knew how to do it well.

The whole mess has made Rikon even skinnier. His six foot four frame is almost impossible to see sideways. His black hair is thick and greasy from too little care and sleep. "As you can see this is all going to take a lot longer than we thought," he says.

Looking around, "No fucking kidding. The insurance isn't enough is it?"

"Ansley I was wondering if you'd just...let me out of the lease. I think I'd just like to cut my losses."

"What! You're making a ton here Rikon. I know this is fucked but –"

"You don't understand Ansley. Pam is pregnant."

"Pregnant, I...I saw her last week. Can't be too far along."

"Not the point. All of this. This club life. Late nights and craziness and now the violence."

"*Vandalism* Rikon. Not violence. No one got hurt."

"Thankfully no one was here to get hurt."

Ansley thinks a moment for an argument. "Rikon when I met you that day you were a nice guy who was bored and suddenly had some money. You wanted a little excitement. Some pizzazz. Well you got the zazzz baby! You run one of the hottest clubs in the hottest of lands. You can't just go."

"Ansley remember that day we met you talked about honest guys. You know – religious guys who repress and want to taste some of the 'prohibited' as you called it. Remember that part of our drunken conversation?"

Ansley nods.

"Well truth is you are what you are Ansley. You can want to jump in an orgy to see what it's like. You can even like it. But in the end you're an orgy man or you aren't. And I am a Lutheran family man.

"Look I like that you helped me break out of a shell. But for a guy like me breaking out of the shell just shows me how much I love the shell. Actually, I *need* the shell Ansley." He takes a step toward Ansley. "Will you let me out?"

Ansley closes his eyes. He really likes Rikon – more than Rikon knows. He respects him. He's an honest guy sensing a bad situation arising from Ansley's dishonesty. Ansley feels like a bastard. The bringer of bad bad things.

"Give it a week," Ansley says. "If you want out I'll set you up right. You're gonna walk away fine from all this Rikon. You have my word."

Rikon seeks out Ansley's eyes to thank him, but he just turns from him and leaves.

Outside it is near twilight and the air is cool on Clubland's carless street. He spots Siema trailing him with fake modesty. Tonight she is wearing a tight red skirt and black blouse. Blue sneakers – no pretense is worth hurting feet. Ansley admires this.

He feels sick about Rikon, about Connery, about himself. He needs something and looks back at Siema. He smiles at her. He needs something and she could really be something.

∼

Like Ansley, Siema enjoys fast cars. She is trailing him now in a black corvette. The streets are wet and the sky is fading from day blue to evening black.

Ansley smiles in his rearview at Siema more than once. She smiles back. They've developed an elaborate flirting ritual consisting of her tailing him around town in fast cars, and then they smile at each other from a distance in bars and clubs. Often the smiles are wry and unusually communicative for two people who've never spoken a word to one another.

Joey has told Ansley more than once to just get it over with and talk to her. So has Randy. But Ansley is enjoying the flirting at a distance and plus, he's afraid. For all the coolness he tries to sell, he's still a dude that dreads failing at impressing a pretty girl. And the more they've danced at a distance, the bigger the first meet has gotten in his head.

But enough is enough and Ansley is ready to end the flirtation thing tonight. At a red light he decides to get out and walk toward her car. It's a quick light and so green hits fast and horns start blowing.

"Greetings," he says. "No need to wonder about my movements tonight. I'll be at Peramo's. A nice private table in back."

Siema is uneasy but never loses her smile. "That's a nice place." Horns are still constant. "Did you plan this?"

Smiling, "No. And I don't need a reservation. They know me. And to know me is to give me the best private table in the house." He turns toward the honking horns. "Thank you red light hostages for making this gesture of mine even more romantic!"

A fat trucker yells, "Fuck you jagoff!"

"And fuck *everybody*!" Ansley yells back. Looking at Siema, "I'm in love. Or at least some honorable lust. Will you attend dinner me-lady?"

Siema hides her face for a moment. This probably shouldn't happen but she says anyway, "Get back in your car Ansley and let's go eat."

∽

"R<small>ED WINE FOR THE LADY</small>," Ansley says.

Peramo's is unusually quiet tonight, which means it's still around 90 percent capacity. The host, William, loves Ansley because Ansley always tips him. Still that isn't enough to get the best table. The owner, Tomas, is also a club leaser. A blackmailed club leaser.

Siema is impressed by the table. It is nicely tucked away in back, discreetly guarded by some large expensive plants. You cannot hear other tables and they can't hear you. It's the perfect date table and it costs twice as much as any of the others. Ansley wouldn't be paying though. The bill would be added to his nonexistent tab.

Peramo's décor is boringly tasteful: dim lighting, soft browns and reds. But its Italian food is wonderful thanks to an amazing chef whose name Ansley cannot pronounce.

"Red wine for the lady," Ansley repeats. "And red wine for the dude."

The waiter gives a mock smile and then departs. Waiters find Ansley amusing since he tips the hell out of them.

Siema sips her water and then, looking at Ansley, forms a smile. "You do make an impression everywhere you go Ansley."

"You know I have kinda built this whole meeting thing up between us. So I am a bit freaked out right now."

"You seem your usual cocky self."

"Well women don't give points for nervous hands do they?"

"It depends on the woman Ansley," Siema says and then waits as the server pours their wine and exits. "Why were you nervous to meet me? I've been following you for a while and you're a cocky SOB."

"Maybe it's all an act."

"It's an act alright. Still you're a cocky SOB."

"So what's your act?"

"What do you mean by that?"

"Who do you work for? Who sent *you*?"

"I know you know that Ansley."

"I know of an idea of a person. Someone very spooky. I don't have a name. And all I know is this man wishes to do me harm."

"A lot of people have you followed."

"And they all want to do me harm."

"Maybe he's just doing research."

"No. He's sent many a beautiful woman to follow me. And they all were dressed up to do me harm. Do you mind if I smoke?"

"Yes. But you're gonna do it anyway."

Ansley drops his cig pack on the table and then, thinking better of it, pulls his hand away, smiling. He raises his glass instead and Siema obliges his toast.

"Fuck for now who you work for," he says. "Fuck for now my smoking. So what did you do before following me around?"

"I was in the military."

Ansley cannot connect the elegant creature before him with army fatigues and morning drills. If it's a lie it's a bold one. "You look like a debutante. There's no tomboy near you. You're the type of chick Scott Fitzgerald wrote about. You want me to believe you were in the army?"

"Marines," Siema says. "In the Gulf War I was part of a special squad that deactivated IED's."

Smiling, "I am not believing this."

Smiling back, "Well it's true."

"And they just let you into combat."

"Have you ever been in a war Ansley?"

"Well I spent a few months in a hippie commune in Georgia."

"Well a lot of shit happens in a war that isn't supposed to." She leans a bit closer. "I am not going to lie to you tonight. I just am not always going to answer you. I was a Marine who deactivated IED's." She leans back. "I'm also a girl who looks incredibly good in this dress. It's why I was perfect for this job."

"I'm the job huh."

"Right now you're the boy who is paying for dinner. I want to start with the garlic rolls."

"Garlic rolls. The smelly way to a girl's heart."

"I am not sleeping with you tonight Ansley."

"Not tonight implies there is a tonight in the future."

"We might never meet again Ansley. So tonight could really mean I am never sleeping with you."

Ansley loves that she isn't easy in any way. He raises his glass for another toast. And then they order.

Looking her over closely, "I am wondering what kind of pop song you are. You know I think people can have their essence distilled into a pop song. Or at least chicks can."

"Well I can't wait to hear what kind of chick I am, Ansley. Now refill my wine glass."

∼

ANSLEY ASKS, "You know what I think will be fun? I'll ask the questions right away you won't answer."

Siema grabs a garlic roll. "Go for it."

"Who is The Man Behind the Curtain?"

"Pass."

"How did you meet him?"

"Do you think my military background has anything to do with it?"

"Yes. Yes I do."

"You're right. But that's all you're gonna be right about there."

"Am I in danger?"

"Tonight?"

"Sure let's start there."

"No. I am not sleeping with you. Remember?"

"So sex with you is dangerous?"

Siema grins. Pinches off a piece of garlic bread and tosses it in her mouth. "I guess you've been doing it wrong. Sex is always dangerous Ansley. When it's right anyway."

"Are you Muslim?"

"Christian. Catholic. Dad is Muslim. Mom is Irish Catholic. I went with mom on religion."

Ansley is amazed and excited that his guess about her youth is right. He wants to tell her but that ain't the right move so he moves on. "You have your mom's Irish blue eyes don't you?"

Smiling, "Yes."

"And what of your dad do you have?"

"A Muslim proclivity for exactitude."

"That's one of the scariest things a woman has ever said to me."

"You may keep asking questions until our entrees arrive."

"Then what?"

"Then I ask you questions Ansley. And we eat of course."

∼

SIEMA'S PORK Ragu is delicious. She lets Ansley taste it and he lets her taste his Pasta and Meatballs. Extra sauce. They're both very happy with the food.

Ansley pours them another glass of wine.

Siema says, "This bottle is much better than the last. And the last was great! This is all so good Ansley. Thank you. I sense there's a gentleman in there even if you are kind of an ass."

"Thank you Siema for calling me a gentleman. When a mysterious woman who may or may not be assigned to kill you calls you a gentleman – you know she means it."

"So how long have you known Joey?"

This sharpens Ansley. She has not used the names of his friends. The question is obviously business. "Oh you know. Don't you?"

"And you're friends? Buds. Bros."

"No."

"So you just put your whole life's wellbeing in a spook you're not friends with?"

"Sure. Why not? That's how this white boy rolls."

"This is a time Ansley you'd do better with the gentleman part rather than the cocky ass."

Ansley looks into Siema's blue eyes. She is not like Connery at all. Where Connery was soft and indecisive, she is hard and sure of herself. Connery was a cute girl with some Irish tomboy in her and a button nose hiding a general confusion and fear of where to land. Siema is beautiful, elegant – and also a tomboy but with no sign of tomboy on her. And if she has confusion and fear Ansley is sure she isn't looking to him for help.

"Ok me-lady. Why are you talking of Joey?"

"You're very smart Ansley."

"Am I?"

"You know you're smart."

"You know what I think? I think people all over this fucking city think I'm smart. Where really I just might be crazy."

"No," Siema says and takes a sip of wine. "You're not crazy. You're just desperate Ansley. And lonely."

Their eyes meet and Siema almost says one thing but his eyes make her say, "But everyone is desperate and lonely, so why not us too?"

∼

THEY WALK NOW on the beach. In the background the lights of Clubland roar. The ocean is black as the night over it. Both are calm.

Ansley reaches for Siema's hand but she pulls away.

"I see," he says.

"Ansley do you want my help?"

"Sure. Tell me who The Man Behind the Curtain is."

"What's an interesting story?"

Ansley is annoyed. "A beautiful Arabic Irish girl breaks her promise *not* to sleep with me."

"You want my help –"

"With cryptic little bon mots?"

"Isn't that what you do to people?"

"Yes and I hate it when it's done to me!"

"I can't tell you who The Man Behind the Curtain is. But I can tell you an interesting story I heard."

Ansley stops walking. Takes a seat on the sand. "Ok. We have no campfire but the ocean should do just fine for a story."

"It's a movie. Kind of." Siema sits and smiles at first but the smile recedes as her words come out. "You love movies and in your – I don't know – to me it's desperation –you try to make your life one. What if a guy like you Ansley – a guy with his head in the clouds trying to live like a movie – had everything he cared for, one by one, removed? What if that were the inciting action used to drive a movie you don't know you're in?"

Ansley thinks of Rikon. Then Randy and Jen. "How in danger are my people Siema?"

"It's not just the people that you care for Ansley," Siema says. "Think of it this way: Someone is trying to force a movie on you. And believe me it's not a comedy. Now what kind of movie will you try to make it instead? A revenge story Ansley? Or a survivor's tale?"

"Just say what you fucking want to say Siema. Tell it to me straight. Without metaphors."

Siema's face turns noticeably frustrated. She wants to say more but can't. Saying more now might do more harm than good. So she rises and says, "I'm going home."

Ansley whispers, "Is that a metaphor?"

"Goodnight Ansley."

"I'll walk you to the garage."

"No," she says. "I'm going home is girl code for the man to leave the girl alone for the night."

Siema starts to walk away and Ansley calls to her, "In this story – this *movie* – are we just for tonight or is there gonna be another tonight?"

Not looking back, "Goodnight Ansley. Walk outside your barn tomorrow at noon."

∼

Hot noon.

Ansley walks over to Siema's sleek black corvette. "Good ride. But let's take mine instead."

Siema looks at his car. It looks wonderful in the sunlight with the top down. "I meant to ask you about that. What kind of car is it?"

Ansley grins. "You definitely have to sleep with me to even have a chance of me answering that."

"What is the big mystery Ansley?"

"That's my affair woman."

"Oh the hell with it."

Siema gets in his mysterious car. Ansley stands in front of the hood and stares at her.

"Ah – you getting in freak? What are you doing standing there staring at me?"

"I just can't help it. In the afternoon sun – with those perfect clouds behind you and that blue sky. You're just so beautiful Siema."

Siema opens her mouth to launch a cynical retort. But the sincerity of Ansley's blue eyes stops her. "Thank you Ansley."

Ansley rolls his eyes, pouting.

"What now!"

"I thought you'd tell me I was pretty since I told you you were pretty."

"Oh fuck off and get in the car!"

"Such language. Maybe you were a Marine."

"I was. Get in the fucking car."

Ansley finally gets in the car and starts it.

"Where are we going Ansley?"

"To introduce you to my friends."

∼

THEY ARE SITTING at Tony's Big Big Big Diner. Jen and Randy are on one side of a booth, Ansley and Siema the other.

Ansley has ordered an assortment of food for the table. Pancakes, waffles, eggs, hamburgers, stuffed mushrooms, tacos, mozzarella sticks and a nacho plate. Randy protested the enormous order but Jen didn't mind – she has a helluva appetite and never gains a pound. She is sipping on a chocolate milkshake and sizing Siema up. So far, she does not like her.

Randy has no reading on Siema. He's more scared of what Ansley is reading into Siema.

"So now that some our food is here let's get down to it," Ansley says. "Siema here – pretty thing isn't she?" He stops for conformation.

Siema rolls her eyes. Randy and Jen nod uneasily.

"Well pretty Siema here is either the arbiter of my doom. And of course *your dooms* by proxy. Or the only hope I have to save Clubland. In simpler words she's our death or saving angel. Helluva opening huh!"

"What do you mean save Clubland?" Jen says and gives Siema a dirty look. "No offense but who the fuck are you?"

Siema rolls her eyes toward Ansley. "Ansley what the hell are you doing?"

"Well Siema technically you do work for the guy who took out Rikon's club. And he has other bad plans for me." Turning back toward Randy and Jen, "He's making a movie out of my life."

"A movie?" Randy asks and looks around for cameras. "You mean a documentary?"

"No Randy. A movie. A movie without any cameras. See this Mr. Big is fucking with me for what seems to me, no reason. And lovely Siema here is assigned to follow me around and tell him god knows what."

"Then why is *she* even here now!" Jen demands.

"I really wish this was a smoking establishment," Ansley says. "I could use a good cig."

Siema tries to leave but she's on the inside of the booth and Ansley stops her. "Siema just be patient. You'll see I have a special genius sometimes."

"You're an asshole Ansley. Nothing special about that."

"So it goes. Look Siema: I don't think you want to hurt me. I think there's a lot more to you than The Man Behind the Curtain has seen. That's why I brought you here to meet Jen and Randy." Turning toward them, "Guys – I trust her."

Randy's face drops. "You trust her…" he whispers.

"I don't!" Jen yells, glaring at Siema. "You need to get your head out of your ass Ansley."

Ansley clears his throat. "Things are going to get worse guys before they get better. Let's not pussyfoot that. Aren't they Siema?"

Siema closes her eyes for a moment. Opening them, "Yes. You're very good Ansley at guessing plots. But I only know pieces. You understand? I don't know what the whole story is or its endgame." Looking at Jen, "I don't want to hurt anyone. Right now I am just following Ansley around. A lot of people follow him around."

"Not who work for the fucker who destroyed Rikon's club," Jen says.

Randy wants to say something but he's got nothing.

Ansley is annoying all of them with how relaxed he has become. He digs into some waffles. "These waffles are made from scratch. They're amazing. Two big things guys to dwell on: It's going to get worse before it gets better. And I trust Siema."

His eyes suddenly trail off and his voice goes deep and serious. "And Siema I need your help or else a lot of people will get hurt. It's not a game for me. Not this time. Despite what you think."

Siema looks at him and then at Randy and Jen. She can't tell them the truth. And there's no lie they'll believe. And her instinct is to think Ansley's professed trust in her is just a move in the game. Her heart has ceased to work on instinct however. It believes him. She thinks, He can't really be this open and vulnerable. No one can be this stupid or crazy or alive.

∼

EVEN THE BEST spooks find it difficult to figure out where Joey lives. Many have decided it's likely he lives with whatever chick(s) he hooks up with that night. He keeps a locker at the gym which presumably holds his clothes and other bits of self.

Right now Joey is exiting his latest conquest. He's spent a lazy day at her place but it's getting dark now and he has business in Clubland. When he gets to his car Siema is leaning against it.

"We need to talk," she says.

∼

THEY SIT IN JOEY'S BENTLEY. The radio reports on a house drug raid gone wrong – the second time in two months the local DEA has gotten the address wrong and frightened a normal family.

Joey turns down the radio. "Fucked up."

Siema asks, "How much are you against him? All in? Or just the percentages they're making you be?"

"This is pointless."

Eyeing him closely, "Is it? Joey I don't know what exact part of The Machine you work for –"

"You work for The Man don't you? So why I am not asking you if you're against Ansley?"

Smirking, "This is gonna take forever Joey if you're going to pretend I don't have another employer. We're both in the same business."

"We can pretend whatever you like. Most of our jobs is pretend Siema. But if you are like me, you ain't gonna tell me shit. And if you're like me – you know I can't tell you fucking shit. Because we both work for The Machine Siema. So why are you bothering me with a morality play?"

"I came here to look you in the eye. I wanna see if you really are the sonuvabitch I think you are."

"Are you falling for Ansley? He's a good guy. He really is. But his head is in the clouds. And he's used all kinds of evil ways to keep it there."

"You give Ansley old blackmail info and access. You use Ansley's access and Clubland to get new assets and better blackmail info. That's the game right?"

"The United States government uses Clubland, Siema."

Looking around his car, "And I guess you take his payoffs. I'm sure Ansley's financed this nice car of yours."

Smirking, "Fuck off Siema. Every spook runs backend deals. You think a government pension is gonna cut it?"

"Do you even like Ansley?"

Joey's eyes flutter a moment. "Like's got nothing to do with it. Clubland allows us to compromise people easily. It's all about collecting intel and assets, Siema."

"And The Man who is after him is a more important asset than Ansley."

Joey sighs. "You know what he snakes back to. And he wants to fuck with Ansley."

"Why! Why the fuck does he care about a weirdo like Ansley?"

Joey stares out the window. The night traffic is picking up. "You're really falling for him aren't you?"

"Answer me Joey."

"There's a streak of good in Clubland. I mean Ansley has criminals running the clubs because let's face it – they're the best ones to handle that business. And he blackmails them. But the business owners below the clubs. Ansley has interrupted the normal flow of the world when it comes to these people."

Turning his head toward Siema, "The world usually stomps on these people. It stomped on Ansley. He's supposed to be an orphan with no prospects and too much booze. But this Benton dude interrupted the world from crushing him and now he's interrupting the world from crushing those weirdos and losers."

"I always wondered if the Benton story was true or if you created it."

"No it's true. And The Man Behind the Curtain, he's evil Siema. The world is run by psychopaths like him. Half of them worship weird pagan gods. I am an atheist by the way. I think all religion is just silly bullshit. Old silly bullshit at that.

"But these fuckers believe in black magic and other weird shit. And psychopaths like a predictable world where they win and misery wins out. Ansley is allowing the meek to inherit the earth. Or at least Clubland. That can't be allowed."

"This is all about those crazy business owners?"

"It's about Ansley," Joey says. "It's about Ansley."

"This is insane."

"You're dealing with insane people who have a lot of money."

"Are they going to kill him?"

"Psychopaths would prefer to kill his heart."

"And that's Clubland."

"Yeah. His heart and soul."

Siema's blue eyes lock onto Joey. "Can you delay it?"

Shaking his head, "No."

"Will you help me then?"

"We work for different floors of the same Machine. We have the same agenda. Intel and assets. Be practical Siema. You know you'll be at best fired if you help him. And our jobs don't just fire people Siema."

"You've known him for a while. He's been great to you. Don't you feel anything Joey for Ansley. *Anything*."

Joey looks off her intense stare. "Yeah," he says. "And when The Machine gives a shit about feelings you let me know."

"You're a psychopath."

"No I just work for the biggest one: The United States government. So do you."

Siema pushes the door open. It's starting to rain. "Fuck you Joey."

"Welcome to The Machine, Siema," he says.

∼

CLUBLAND IS ESPECIALLY alight tonight and Ansley stands in the middle of the peopled street, watching balloons drift by. A lot of them say, Happy Birthday. And a lot of them say, Look Above if you want God to look Below.

It took some real talent to get that sentence on a balloon.

Ansley closes his eyes. Steadies himself. He can feel the energy of Clubland drawing him in. And then eyes are open and he is walking, smiling and ass slapping his way across The Horseshoe. He goes into every club, hears R&B and techno and rock and disco. He experiences every kind of music and every kind of smile. And then, in Club Rager, he sees Siema, her back arched in a one piece blue dress. It shows a lot of leg. Her heels are blue as well and she's dabbed some seductive blue eye shadow on. No lipstick, but Siema's lips are naturally seductive – anything artificial on them just takes away rather than adds.

Siema walks toward him. The techno music is blasting and she yells, "We need to go somewhere quiet!"

Ansley smiles. He knows just the place.

∼

SEASHELLS IS QUIET TONIGHT. Lara is bartending. She recently moved here, fleeing a bad post college relationship and looking for a job in Clubland. Ansley took a liking to her instantly and decided her pop song would have a country flavor. Probably because she has a lovely southern drawl.

Ansley got Lara a job in Clubland on the condition that she take the job he got her bartending at Seashells once a week. He also got her a place to stay. A small apartment not too far from Clubland. He paid the rent for a year and didn't tell her. She knows anyway.

Why did he want her to bartend one night at this dive? Lara thought maybe he just likes seeing her in a place he actually drinks. This is true – but Ansley feared that Clubland wouldn't be for her and yet she'd have to stay there because of the money. So he built in a forced reprieve from it.

Lara is very intelligent. She has recently enrolled back in school to get her masters in nursing. And she has a great rack. All these things Ansley admires about her.

He met her in Clubland the day after Connery left for the farm. And although he thought about hitting on her – she is a girl he could love – something suggested friends as opposed to star crossed lovers. So he did what he always does when confronted with a woman he thinks needs saving: He tried to fix her life.

Lara kinda adores Ansley. He's a lovable asshole and perhaps because her father is a lovable asshole, she has a soft spot for him. She is surprised to see him walk in with a girl – he always comes here alone. And she's very surprised at the beauty and confidence she sees in Siema. She is obviously not a simple club girl.

Ansley always enjoys hearing the southern twang of Lara's voice – it's so sweet and sexy. "How are you Lara?" he says. "I see the rack is ripe as hell tonight."

Siema hits Ansley. Hard. "That's out of line!"

Lara smiles. "It is," she says and Ansley grins at the southern twang. "But I just spit in his beers. So."

Siema can see that Lara likes Ansley. She hasn't met a service industry person that doesn't. "I'll spit in it too," she says.

"Great!" Lara says.

Ansley rolls his eyes. "You two ought to get a room."

He orders a beer and Siema orders a weird drink; he can't grasp what's in it even when Lara explains it.

They find the quietest table.

"So pretty lady. Why are we here?"

"I need to tell you some stuff. It's probably the wrong idea to do so. And it's gonna put me at risk –"

"Gosh you look pretty."

"Ansley please."

"I don't think you should talk. I don't want you to get hurt."

Smiling, "Fuck off. So I met with my boss today."

"The Man Behind the Curtain."
"No Ansley. My real boss."

※

SIEMA'S BOSS is a maker and shaker in the intelligence world. There are over forty intelligence agencies used by the United States government, some of them private. He runs a private firm and unbeknownst to the rest of the agencies, he isn't a psychopath and so doesn't like the way the world is going. Through just luck he met Siema and decided that she would be his perfect spy for The Man Behind the Curtain. So he recommended her to the bastard; her beauty got her hired. He doesn't trust her though and that's why he thought she might work on Ansley – she has a decency that the other beauties didn't.

Sai Siema doesn't know her boss' real name. He uses many monikers. With her he's usually Paul. A small man in his 50's, Paul is one of those guys that always looks like he's wearing a toupee. He's not. But his hair is just one rectangular dark patch that looks like the adhesive is loosening. It always takes everything Siema has to not stare at it. No one would think Paul could be a spy – he barely looks powerful enough to be an accountant.

They met earlier today at a random empty office Paul keeps in town. He was wearing a blue suit that was too big on him. And his hair was as terrible as ever.

Paul was blunt after hearing Siema's story. "I can't protect you if you get too far out in the open. I need to keep up appearances that I am with the Big Plan. If I allow you to help Ansley they'll look sideways at me and soon you'll have a new boss that is crazy like the rest of 'em." He scratched his head and Siema almost giggled because his hair looks like it's about to fall off. She's sure Paul would be better off with a toupee than his real hair. Poor thing.

"The Man Behind the Curtain doesn't trust me, Paul. But he still gave me enough to know he's gonna ruin Ansley."

"He won't kill him unless Ansley makes him mad. He just wants to destroy him. And he wants his clubs."

"I've made my decision Paul." Her blue eyes locked onto him. "I'm gonna help him. Is there a way he can win?"

"No. Not unless you redefine win."

"What do you mean by that?"

"Ask Ansley, Siema. I'll hold onto you long enough to help you. But I will have to burn you. Also, there's the matter of Joey."

"He's a bastard. He won't help."

"Does he know you work for me?"

"After talking with him I think he believes our cover story."

"Joey is an X factor in all this. He's smart enough to figure me out. And that would hurt my other plans. He's practical, not evil. But practical men in this game often let holocausts happen. Play keep away with him for me Siema."

"You got it boss. And thank you."

"This isn't a thing that earns a thanks. This whole mess is not going to be kind to you, Siema. Unless you get very lucky. Take it from an old spook: Pray a lot."

∼

SIEMA HAS FINISHED RELAYING HER BOSS' proclamations.

Ansley has a way of ignoring important stuff if he gets good news on an obsession he has. "I was right about you not being against me. Ha! I am good baby."

"Ansley I could be lying to you. You just believe shit."

Smiling, "Yes I do Siema. Yes I do."

"So. Do you have a plan?"

"Yes. Losing." He waves Lara over. "Lots more booze," he says.

∼

AS ANSLEY and Siema's night drifts into more alcohol, a four man wrecking crew plan their night of destruction. The leader is bald and the streetlamp they've gathered around blasts off his head fiercely. The other three, who have thick manes, try not to look at his shiny head.

"We'll take the balloon shop tonight. And...we'll pick a random restaurant. Maybe some others too. The police won't be a problem. We can take our time."

The other three light cigarettes and nod.

"We'll meet back here at 3am. That's our start time. And remember have three loaded handguns on your person. Tonight it might matter."

∼

Ansley should not have driven home. He lied to Lara about waiting on a cab. When Lara saw Ansley driving away she was pissed.

He usually isn't irresponsible like this but his mind is going at a thousand paces. Siema usually wouldn't have let someone as drunk as Ansley drive her, but she's just as worse for wear as he is.

They are staggering now toward his barn. Both fall at least once. They can't stop laughing.

Once inside, Ansley switches on whatever CD is in the player. Fleetwood Mac. Rumours. He has no recollection of listening to this. And then he pokes at his remote and the place becomes full of strawberry light.

Siema walks around, taking in the empty space as Stevie Nicks sings about broken love. "You live like an orphan who got some money," she says.

Ansley throws a smile her way. His insides are on fire watching her walk – her back perfectly arched, her legs perfectly smooth. This is why you live, he thinks.

Siema allows herself to fall onto his bed. "So are you going to try to sleep with me?"

Ansley's face becomes serious. His plight overtakes her sex for a moment. He crawls into bed next to her and, wordlessly, takes her into his arms. She feels soft and vulnerable against him.

Siema brushes his broad shoulders and then pushes her head

against his chest. Her eyes can't stay open another second and Ansley listens to her worried breathing.

He wonders about the pop song Siema could be. Or is. And why would she want him to hear it? He's sure he doesn't deserve her.

Siema's soul seems too big for a three minute tune. A pop song could never distill the beautiful feminine wonder sleeping in his arms. But she's too beautiful and wonderful not to have one in her. It's probably a dance song he thinks – a dance song about love. Because writing about her blue eyes over piano keys and adding some sad lyrics aren't enough. No Siema is a mover, a doer. No matter what troubled or sad music life throws at her, she finds a way to dance. She is one of the hardest things in the universe to find: A beautiful girl with a loyal heart and the courage to try.

5

MICE AND MEN AND PLANS

It is the morning after.
Siema finds Ansley sitting in the gazebo's swing. He is not swinging though. He is smoking.

"I'm going to quit," he says. "I don't think I can make cigs a regular part of me. I'm too lazy to be an addict."

Siema is wearing a blue dress shirt of Ansley's – it's long enough to cover half her thighs. "Why don't you come inside and I'll make some breakfast. My mom is an awesome cook. She taught me her secrets."

"You were really out of it. I just put on the radio loud and it didn't budge you. Sometime during the night you woke up and changed into my shirt."

"I was drunk as hell Ansley."

"The radio station did one of their little news breaks. The cops fucked up again and raided a normal family home as if it were a drug house. It's like the third or fourth time now. And oh – several of the businesses in Clubland were destroyed last night."

He takes a puff. "They killed Margaret. Crazy old bat. They had to be ready for her. Or else she would have taken at least one of them out."

Siema kneels beside Ansley, gently touching his shoulders. "Are you ok?"

Looking at her, "No. In some way I am responsible for an old woman's death. I am not ok Siema. They'll kill'em all just to make me responsible. It's me. It's always fucking me."

"You are not responsible for this. Evil is. You're dealing with true evil Ansley. And I don't think you really get that."

"I am the fucker responsible. I treated reality like some silly fucking movie. Except death is forever in real life."

"You saw Clubland's dangers as only affecting you. But you've made a family there Ansley. And that's a beautiful thing. But these people out to get you hate beautiful things. I just don't think you get how awful they are."

"Oh I get it now. But it's still *me* Siema. Don't you fucking get it? I am bad karma. I am an orphan who should never get close to anyone."

Siema holds his face. "That's fucking bullshit. You're kind. And they hate you because you're a kind person. They're evil. So fuck them and don't let them break you."

Ansley gently removes her hands from his face. He does hold onto them for a bit. Siema is sure he's going to let it out, that'll he finally let down his guard enough to cry. But the orphan in him stops short and releases her hands from his grip.

"I gotta go in for a meeting with the shop owners. I gotta talk to them."

"You want me to go with you?"

"No. I want you to stay with my plan of giving up gracefully. And I decided I don't want your help. Just stay the fuck out of this. I don't want you dead."

"You know that's not happening. You are gonna need me to win this. And we can win this Ansley."

Ansley sighs. Flicks his cigarette butt and then looks into Siema's soft blue eyes. He tells her she's right. It's a necessary lie.

∽

Ansley's cavalcade of freaks and losers gather at Rich's Mama Good restaurant. He serves biscuits and water. Rich isn't much on free buffets.

His place has been left untouched by last night's violence. They did take out Margaret's balloon shop, Pat's Foot in Mouth and Julie Nesmar's Little Cats – which is a French cuisine restaurant that has nothing to do with cats. And of course they killed crazy old Margaret.

All of the freaks are yelling at Ansley. They aren't grateful to him for helping them get their businesses. But Ansley discovers everyday that gratitude is a rare commodity.

People who have had success wouldn't let this situation unravel them. They might act as if the sky is falling, but inside they would know they have the wits and resolve to overcome and succeed – if not in Clubland then someplace else. But Ansley's fucked up crew knows that Clubland is it for them.

Ansley gazes at the mob before him. Hair ranges from none to blue to 80's teased. Pants range from denim to vinyl. Shirts and blouses go from garage sale to Armani. Some are young, some are old, all are scared. And desperation always leads to accusation.

"This is your goddamn fault!" Rich screams. He bites into a biscuit.

Pat yells, "Margaret is dead because of you!"

Julie Nesmar yells, "What are you fucking gonna do about this you fucker!"

The whole crowd starts to yell out profanities, their shouts merging to make an angry music.

"We're not gonna just fucking stand here and let them kill us!"

"Ansley you done fucked up big this time you asshole!"

"We're all gonna be dead because of *you* you crazy sonuvabitch."

On and on it continues like this until Ansley finally blows.

"Fuck all you people!" he screams so loudly his voice cracks. He stands on a table. Bites into a biscuit and then throws the rest of it at the mob.

He yells, "All you fucking freaks wouldn't be anywhere without me! You ungrateful losers. I was never ungrateful to Benton. And I was a loser when he helped me. Fuck I'm still a loser. And I might be an asshole but I'm better than you fucking whack jobs!"

He jumps down. "Yeah I am a loser like you freaks. But I got lucky. And you all got lucky that I got lucky. And what you fucking assholes can't see is the world at large doesn't like losers like us getting lucky. Got it? So if you want to keep your places you're gonna have to look in the mirror and say: I am a loser. I got lucky. And now I gotta do whatever it takes to hold onto this luck. Even if that means burning it down."

Ansley begins to pace like a general giving a briefing.

"If you think holding onto luck when you're born luckless is easy – well fuckers think again! It's as hard as holding onto love and let's face it – all of us here have fucked that up. You can't buy luck you fucking assholes. That's handed down by God and taken away by God. What God wants from us we won't know until the story's over."

Ansley picks up another biscuit. "Rich you're a cheap fucker. You didn't even put out butter for the biscuits."

He takes a bite and then a big gulp of water. "Listen up you fuck sticks: You wanna keep this little unreality I've built? Then you're gonna do exactly what I say. Or else you can all go fuck about and I'll leave you all to waste down to the born loser shitheads you really are."

Ansley looks around. The mob has turned inward. For a few moments it's as quiet as a wake.

"The good news," Ansley finally says, "is you aren't going to have to win to win. With my plan you can be your natural loser selves. And fuck off if you think I am telling you sad assholes my plan."

~

AT MIDNIGHT ANSLEY meets with three fellas who have efficiently handled nasty business for him in the past. They are all tall, quiet, and untraceable.

"Remember," he instructs, "do not burn down any more of the

businesses and clubs than I've listed. We need some ash. But not ashes."

∽

THE NEWS LEADS with the major fires at Clubland last night. And the press has gathered in the car-less street for Ansley's official statement on it.

Ansley now knows the name of The Man Behind the Curtain. He hasn't told anyone – especially Siema, that he knows. How he got it is a story of luck and looking for luck. And since God hands down luck, Ansley is sure God wants him to have it and use it.

And now he stands, wearing a pink suit, white shirt and blue loafers, before a dozen reporters. In back of him is the limited ash he ordered. The reporters take in the extent of the damage – all fires look bad so it's a great visual aid for Ansley now.

He looks into the cameras and microphones. "As you know Clubland has had a bad run of luck lately. And this is putting a strain on us financially. But the good that Clubland provides this community is so important that a major benefactor – a man with deep pockets and a deeper heart that has nothing but concern and joy for his fellow man.

"This man has agreed to finance the repairs and the security of Clubland. This man, who can only be called a saint, has agreed that in five years, his ownership stake that I've sold him will transfer into a sort of co-op for the businesses here. Clubland will be owned and run by its wonderful eclectic businesses. All parking profits will then go to Sister Heart's Orphanage. And I know this man is as proud as I am not only to *not* make a dime off this. But to also finance the entire process."

Ansley looks into the cameras but sees only his foe. "The man I speak of is Gordon Chenosti. An immigrant. A survivor of the Holocaust. A businessman who sees money as just paper that makes dreams come true."

He smiles at his foe.

"Gordon Chenosti. I thank you. And I can't wait to see you."

∼

When Siema sees the news she calls her boss.

"Paul – Ansley's fucked."

"He saved you though. You're still in full cover. You can walk. And he wants you to walk Siema. He's come out into the open alone. Let me help you out of this. I can pull you away from The Man. Ansley's insanity is perfect cover."

"He lied to me about his plan. Except for the losing part. I don't even know if he has a plan, Paul. He's baiting Chenosti. I don't think Ansley has a second move here. He always believes he'll just make one up when he has to."

Paul has been in the spook game for a long time – men lying to women to protect them is not unusual. "He's doing what men do," Paul says. "Just don't let it go to waste. He's trying to protect you."

Siema doesn't want to hear this. "Fuck protection Paul. I am not coming in from the cold on this."

She hangs up the phone angrily and thinks: It's Ansley that really needs protection. From himself.

∼

Ansley avoids seeing Siema after the news conference. For obvious reasons.

It is midnight and he sits in an empty diner. His food is untouched. The only alcohol on the menu is domestic beer and he considers ordering one, but he notices an impeccably dressed man walking toward him. Blonde. Tall. Black suit.

"Mr. Ansley," he says. "Mr. Chenosti saw your press conference. A car is waiting for you. Do not worry about the meal. I will take care of that."

Ansley grins at him for a moment, lets the silence marinate. "I think I'd rather drive my own car."

Grinning back, "Unfortunately your car is not operational."

Ansley loses his grin; he is pissed. They didn't just fuck with his life – his precious mysterious car is a casualty too! He knows he's never going to see her again.

"Ok. I see. I trust you'll take great care of my car."

Smiling, "It's being handled thoroughly as we speak."

Ansley tries to put on his best poker face. But the "handled thoroughly as we speak" part stings. "Is it a long drive?" he asks.

The tall blonde man in black remains motionless for a moment. "Not if you have something to think about," he says.

~

ANSLEY ISN'T SURPRISED to be driven to an opulent mansion full of palm trees and pools, inside and out. The gate which guards it is military grade and the men who guard the gate are also military grade. They hide their weapons well in their expensive suits and good manners. But their eyes are always exacting, as if measuring the shot.

Ansley is guided to a modest study room, given the opulence of the rest of the place. It is small with a fireplace that is useless in tropical weather – the room is extra cooled so it can be fired on. Two large red chairs sit on opposite ends of a handcrafted wood table which has a handcrafted wood chess set sitting on it.

In one of the red chairs sits Gordon Chenosti. The light of the fire inconsistently illuminates his expressionless face.

Ansley takes his time looking him over. He's in his 70's, he's got a bit of a belly and laughable, long white hair styled in a bowl cut. He looks like someone who never left the Swinging London of the 60's. But his eyes are large green ovals which see the world as prey to be determined. He wears a red smoking jacket which perfectly matches the red chairs. He sips now what appears to be red wine and modestly toasts Ansley. He does not offer Ansley a drink.

Ansley's escort leaves them and Ansley sits in the red chair across from Gordon. He looks into his predatory eyes. Not a hint of human emotion can be found.

Ansley can tell Gordon is expecting him to break the silence. So he doesn't. He smirks instead.

Gordon is trying to seem casual. But Ansley knows this is anything but a casual meeting and is shocked he'd make such a false opening move.

Finally Gordon gestures to the chess board. "I had it brought in here for you. I don't play the game."

"It would seem Gordon you play a lot of chess. With real people as pawns and who the hell knows what you use for the good pieces."

Smiling, "Your press conference was unexpected. You've been unexpected all throughout this though."

"Did you like the part where I went over multiple legal firms and government agencies – as well as the press – having full access to all our financials? To show the public we're all about charity and honesty. I really liked that one."

"Ansley you strike me as a man who would know that the press is an entity owned not operated. And lawyers and governments never offer real protection unless you're the highest bidder."

"Or blackmailer."

Gordon's voice deepens, "You are neither."

Ansley nods. Thinks a moment and then leans toward him, "Guys like you Gordon always have it all. Yet you people are never satisfied with winning though. You need victims. You need souls don't you. Just like the devil you worship."

He leans back into a comfortable pose. "You're not human. I used to wonder if I was but I must be because you wouldn't go thru all this trouble to destroy me if I wasn't. I guess it's a compliment if the devil finds your soul worth coveting."

Gordon takes a sip of his red wine. "No souls are worth coveting Ansley. They're too cheap and easy to get. And I doubt you'll find your future complimentary."

"I did you a solid today Gordon. I kinda gave you Clubland. Well gave it to you so you could very publicly rebuild it and then give it away to the losers and freaks. But I made you look good."

Gordon points to the pristine chess board. "If we were to play a game – what do you think would happen?"

"You mean to my life?"

"No. Within the game."

"I guess I'd take some pieces and you'd take some pieces and since neither of us play chess someone would accidentally win."

"Yes. Perfectly said. One of us would accidentally win. But that's not what would happen."

Ansley looks at the chessboard again.

Gordon interrupts him before he can speak. "You see whether the pieces stay on the board or come off doesn't matter. That's just the part you can see."

Gordon's evil eyes tell Ansley now that this has become personal for him. Ansley has really pissed him off. This is no longer some evil abstract exercise. It's revenge.

Gordon takes a gulp of wine. "You have been living with the idea that if you just make the right moves this thing is winnable. You might play our chess game as a mouse or a man. But it'll never be winnable for you Ansley. You think you're playing, but really we're the only ones making any moves. And we're so good at convincing you that you're playing that you never figure that out. You call your ignorance *hope*."

Ansley takes a moment to think about Gordon's soliloquy. "I must have really spanked you to get this meeting and for you to give me that speech. You need me to know the face who destroyed me. I made you care huh."

Gordon's predatory green eyes look off Ansley. He feels his way down the right side of his chair, pushes a button and instantly the room is filled with five bodyguards. Politely but firmly they lift Ansley out of the chair. Gordon stares emotionless at him, his smile small, but sure.

Ansley's instinct is to say Fuck You. But he sees Randy and Jen and beautiful Siema. He knows Gordon is right: he has no moves to make because he never had any moves. If he pisses him off more, Gordon might go after everyone he cares for, including Connery. He might do it anyway. Evil isn't satisfied until all know their soul is lost.

Something about Gordon's face changes now – the light of the fire seems to draw out all the hate inside of him, which vacuums his skin tight like a snake's. He looks like what he is – a demon poorly wearing a human suit. And he waves Ansley away now. He chooses no parting words. It's a final cold spit on Ansley's soon to be grave.

∼

Ansley is driven to a safe house. Although blindfolded, he's sure the place is big enough and hidden enough to soundproof his death.

When the blindfold is removed Ansley sees the five bodyguards who took him out of Gordon's mansion. But he also sees a short fellow. Maybe five four with dark hair. His face is the kind that seems so familiar, it's unmemorable.

Ansley is tied impossibly tight to a chair. He surmises that he's in an empty living room except for the chair he's tied to. The windows are covered by thick black drapes. A few dim lights show enough to be scared. He looks to his right and sees one other piece of furniture: a TV tray holding intimidating metal instruments.

The short fellow walks toward him. "I like to keep things direct. You are going to die tonight. But that's not the punchline." He tilts his head toward the intimidating looking instruments. "No the funny part is you're going to be *thankful* to die tonight."

The short fellow turns toward the five bodyguards and makes a gesture. One by one they descend on Ansley and start pummeling.

∼

Getting beaten senseless makes reality akin to dream time. Ansley is not sure if he's been getting beaten for hours or minutes. Blood is everywhere on his face. His eyes are nearly closed from the bruising. He's vomited a few times from the gut punches. He raises his head and sees the short fellow looking at him eye level.

"That's just the overture," he says and turns toward the evil metal on the table.

As he mulls which cold instrument to start with a loud thud is suddenly heard. Then another one and another one. Ansley is sure the sounds are some instrument of torture being prepared. But then he hears angry yelling – serious voices screaming, Get on the fucking ground! Don't fucking move or you fucking die!

And suddenly Ansley is aware that the short fellow is no longer standing before him. He is cowering now on his knees. A large man in black tactical gear points a scary shotgun at his head. Through his battered eyes Ansley makes out the letters DEA on his bullet proof vest.

Ansley realizes the local DEA has fucked up another address. Bloodied and broken, he looks at the short fellow and aches out, "Deus ex machina."

6

SIDEWALKS

It is Joey who notifies Randy about Ansley's hospitalization. He immediately picks up Jen and heads to the hospital. And Joey finds Siema at Ansley's barn. He drives her in silence to the hospital.

All of them are horrified at Ansley's appearance. His face is mangled, his ribs broken. He's incoherent from all the morphine.

Joey tries a joke. "Bud I met your doctor. He's Asian. And Jewish. You're gonna live!"

Siema says, "Fuck this!" and grabs Joey's arm, dragging him outside for a private meeting.

∼

Siema wastes no time.

"You're helping me," she demands.

Joey rolls his eyes. "Siema the cops picked up the guys who beat him. The head torturer isn't much on loyalty. He rolled on The Man Behind the Curtain. The police raided his mansion and found his kiddie stuff. You don't need to do anything."

"Fuck you Joey. He's going to get off."

"Not on this."

"Your people will arrange a sweetheart deal. No way. This ends now."

"He doesn't have time to play around with fucking Clubland. He's using everything he has to make this a minor story in the press. That kiddie porn he stashed is bad. He's in the pics with the kids."

Siema grabs Joey's arm and moves in close, his eyes only inches from hers. "You must have some decency in you. You try to hide your concern but I can see you're worried about Ansley. Now do the right thing and help me kill this disgusting fuck."

Joey shakes loose from her grip. "That won't change anything. People like him are the price of doing business in the world Siema."

"I always hear how taking this guy out or that guy out won't change anything. That's a fucking lie. There'll be one less bastard in the world pulling strings and fucking kids. And it'll end this with Ansley. He was going to fucking kill him Joey."

Joey begins to pace. "If Ansley had just not insisted on playing the game out in the open, he wouldn't be in that hospital bed. He was just going to fuck with him. And take Clubland. When Ansley did that press conference he committed suicide."

"No. He was trying to get out in front of this. He was trying to take me out of the game. And he wanted to save Clubland for the freaks and weirdos."

"Ansley is crazy Siema. And you're nuts for thinking I'd help you murder The Man."

Siema closes distance on Joey again. Eyes to eyes, "You're going to help me kill him. Or you're responsible when he kills Ansley. And fucks another child. Which you and I both know he's going to do. Fucking help me please!"

∾

JOEY AND SIEMA sit at Briner's Diner, talking scenarios over pancakes.

Killing Gordon Chenosti isn't going to be easy. That mansion of his is a fortress. His guards are all military grade killers. There cannot be any sneaking in and doing the deed.

"You see what I mean?" Joey says after a frustrating half hour. "He doesn't go out much. And when he does he's guarded. He's always fucking guarded by guys who know what they're doing. And as soon as he gets this case thru the courts he's never coming back to this state. He'll probably lay low in Africa for a while. Easy kids to score there too."

"He's gotta go. Ansley will never be safe unless he's gone. There is something that occurred to me."

"Speak."

"His attorney is Lewis Morton. He has an office in that weird building. The one with a lot of sidewalks you have to walk down to get to the front door."

"It's a modern art piece of crap."

"How many guards does he take to the lawyer's office?"

"How the hell should I know?"

"Find out. I assume he's still talking to you. We might be able to use that – it could come in handy."

"I'm still a point man on some stuff he's working with us on."

"Great. And you'll have to be stealth and tail him to the lawyer's office."

"Why? I can just rent an office in that building."

"Even better. Let's see how many guards walk him inside. I got a hunch about something."

∽

JOEY GOT LUCKY.

A perfect space for viewing Gordon's entrance was for rent. He got it and now sits in an empty office save for one chair and desk. It's on the tenth floor of a twelve floor building. Since he doesn't know when Gordon will visit his lawyer, he has to spend 9-5 every day for a week sitting and watching. By day seven he wants to kill himself. He's never enjoyed surveillance.

But day seven turns lucky. He spots Gordon walking in, sans bodyguards.

He takes out his Motorola 888 cell phone and calls Siema on the Motorola 888 he gave her. "Meet me at Briner's Diner in one hour."

∼

Traffic is hell but Joey finally pulls into the diner's parking lot. Siema is already there, sitting in her Corvette with the top down.

"We're in luck. He doesn't walk in with *any* bodyguards."

Siema's face begins to beam. "I had a hunch he'd go into the lawyer's office alone. Lawyers and doctors are private things. Fuck – I'll buy the pancakes!"

∼

Siema asks, "The question is do we sniper or take him on the ground?"

"You can't sniper. It's too risky shooting him from the office. Inevitably they'll wanna talk to everyone who had a vantage point to shoot him that rents there. I've rented in a fake name of course. But I can't have any light on me. We have to take him on the ground." He takes a sip of coffee. "Actually you do. When you hear my plan you'll know why it has to be you."

"Fine." Siema's blue eyes don't blink. "I don't care. I'll do it. He's gotta go."

"We need to make you blonde. Wearing sunglasses and a hat. He'll look at you as you saunter near him because he's a perv. So he'll slow his walk. There's a spray that we use that will induce a heart attack. He doesn't have a good ticker by the way. So this will kill him fucking good and quick. You have to get close though to make sure it goes up his nose. Three full squirts."

"Joey just get me the fucking spray."

"And then there's the matter that both of us will be burned if anyone finds out. You can't even tell Ansley. This is a war situation

Siema. You were in one. You and me are soldiers now in battle. And I need from you a soldier's loyalty and silence. Look me in the eye and swear it."

Siema leans forward. Locks her eyes onto his. "I promise you no one but my priest who hears my confession will ever know a fucking thing we do. You have my word and my honor."

The waitress brings over the pancakes.

"These are good pancakes," Joey says. "This is gonna be pretty boring work. You're gonna be sitting in a courtyard for hours watching people walk down long curvy sidewalks into the building."

"What time did he arrive for his lawyer?"

"About 4pm."

"It's Friday. Perhaps this is his usual day. He probably goes every other week for a review on the case. He feels safe there. He wouldn't want to talk over the phone or in his house – probably paranoid about being bugged while the case is active. There are always do-gooder FBI that don't get the memo to leave people like him alone."

"What are you getting at?"

"Try to make plans with him to discuss the shit you are working on with him. Choose a Friday two weeks from today. Say 3-5pm. He might tell you he's busy and we'll get lucky and know where he'll be busy."

Joey chews some pancake thoughtfully. "That's fucking brilliant Siema."

Siema bites into a syrupy pancake. "Only if it works."

∼

NOT ONLY DID Gordon say he is gonna be busy on that Friday, he blurted out to Joey that he's got a legal appointment that day.

Siema takes her time getting ready on the pivotal Friday. She wears a blonde wig and sun hat which look great on her. She chooses black sunglasses which are slightly too large for her – kind of a hippie fashion statement that also will hide her identity well. She makes sure her red skirt is short and tight and her black heels are high. Her white blouse shows plenty of cleavage.

Joey watches thru binoculars from his office space.

The event starts at 2pm – they figure he'll be here at 4pm but don't want to cut it too close. Siema sits on a bench near the small fountain pretending to read. Five minutes till 4pm a lawyer from one of the many legal offices in this building sits next to her holding a sandwich.

"I haven't seen you here before. I'm Mike." He holds out his hand.

Oh God, Siema thinks, he's here to hit on me. She needs to blow him off but not in a way that will cause a scene.

Joey watches thru the binoculars. "Get rid of the asshole!" he shouts.

Mike says, "So I am a partner here at Liff and Burn. Youngest one by the way." He smiles. "Where do you work? And gosh that's a great hat you got on. You look very pretty in it I must say."

Siema checks her watch. Two minutes to 4pm.

"Listen," she says. "I'm pregnant. And I need some free legal advice. I was hoping to meet a handsome lawyer sitting out here. I got no money right now. The adult club fired me when this bitch there outed me as preggers.

"My boyfriend is in jail. Now we hope his public defender can get the fucking charge down to manslaughter. But I am hoping he can get conjugal visits worked in the plea. You think that's possible? I really don't want to be without IT while he's in the slammer. And he'll kill anybody else I'm interested in – that's how he got in the slammer. We're hoping crime of passion will make it manslaughter. What do you think about that too?"

Mike takes a bite of his sandwich. "I'm not a criminal lawyer. I'll see you later."

He's gone in seconds.

Siema takes a deep breath and then sees Gordon walking down the path.

Joey whispers, "Get up and show him the fucking goods. Go go girl."

Siema does just that. She rises and starts to walk Gordon's way. When he stops to check her out she cleverly milks the moment, stopping and pulling her skirt up a few inches higher. Then she looks Gordon's way and says in a southern accent, "Excuse me sir. Can I ask you for some directions? I am just so lost."

She walks toward Gordon and times her high-heels trip so she can fall perfectly into his arms. He enjoys catching her.

"Oh my lord these heels!" Siema says. "Thank you so much for catching me. In my purse I got the address."

She spots three people walking their way.

"Don't play with the food Siema," Joey whispers. "Do it now."

As Gordon's eyes pass over her cleavage, Siema reaches in her purse and pulls out the spray. In one swift motion she sends three solid hits up Gordon's nose. He collapses immediately.

Siema then yells to the three people walking toward her, "Oh my god! He was giving me directions and just passed out! Does anyone know CPR?"

"I do," one man says and a woman with him screams she's going inside to call 911.

"Oh thank heavens!" Siema says.

"Get out of there now Siema," Joey whispers.

People can sense a juicy crisis and at least ten more come running out of the building to gawk. Siema quietly backs away from them. It's a long walk down the curvy sidewalks back to the street and her car. Her adrenaline runs non-stop.

Once in the car she has to take a few deep breaths. Then she pulls into traffic. A half mile down the road there is a Denny's. That's where she's going to meet Joey. During the drive she removes the wig and hat.

Once in the parking lot the reality of what she has just done hits her. It's one thing to shoot at a human being in war. She had done that. It's another to plan and execute a human being's murder. Even if he was evil. And her Catholic heart is drowning now in guilt.

"Forgive me Father," she whispers. "For I have sinned."

7

SEPTEMBER 24, 1994

When Ansley got the news of Gordon's death, he resigned himself to never ask Siema about it. He knew she either did it or had it done. But for a relationship to be successful, you have to know what you don't want to know.

Siema spent every day by Ansley's side, handling the doctors and nurses. Jen and Randy handled the day to day of The Horseshoe. And no one from Clubland visited except for Lara.

Of course the club leasers were hoping Ansley didn't make it – and his dead man switch wasn't real. And the wacko business people he gave hope and purpose, well they're just ungrateful bastards that nevertheless are his cross to bear.

Once discharged from the hospital, Siema and Ansley began an old fashioned courtship. They never formally said they weren't going to jump each other when Ansley became physically capable. Life just happened and all the little things that make up life they shared: meals, movies (Siema bought him a TV and VCR), music, silly arguments.

They told each other their life stories and left out the parts best left out. They slept in the same bed, often awaking in each other's arms. The lack of sex intensified and eroticized their long conversations about love, God, life, purpose. Ansley especially enjoyed their discussions – and often arguments, about music, seeing as he interpreted so much of life thru it.

They shared everything except their bodies. It went unspoken but both understood that marriage was needed for that – somehow, someway they had embraced the idea that they needed to go before God and pledge vows before they could hit the good stuff. Ansley could tell Siema liked being an old fashioned gal. And he didn't mind waiting. Especially if it showed Siema how much he loved her.

And today is the day he bought the ring. But he cannot give it to her yet. A disturbing piece of news has reached him.

"I need to go on a short trip," Ansley tells Siema. "I need you to trust me and not ask me about it. And believe me when I tell you I will hold nothing back once I get back."

Siema is worried and studies his blue eyes – they seem honest, but also sad. "Is this about Clubland –"

"No. I need you to trust me Siema. It's just a few days. I need to check on something. And I promise you I will tell you everything. Do you trust me?"

"When are you leaving?"

"In three days."

"How long?"

"Just for three days."

"And then you tell me what it was about?"

"I'll tell you everything for the rest of my life baby. Trust me?"

"Yes Ansley. I do trust you." Siema hugs him, holds him tight and whispers, "I trust you even though I know you're nuts."

Holding Siema makes Ansley wish time could stop. Every part of his heart and mind is intoxicated by her. He has to find a way to get out of the spotlight to protect her. He has to unload Clubland without harming the wackos and freaks – even if they don't appreciate or like him. There's a streak of good and crazy in Clubland that the world needs and Ansley doesn't want that to vanish. But he's often failed at what he has tried to save. That's why he's going away for three days. He needs to see for himself what has happened to Connery.

8

REPRISE

It's a bumpy flight. Ansley looks out the window but the farmland below is covered by darkness. He tries to imagine vast fields filled with wheat and cows and assorted crops. This is where he sent Connery to reset her life. His imagination had seen her smiling in straw fields, her button nose pressed up against horses and dogs and cats. Her past was finally gone thanks to the unexpected turn he had provided.

But a week ago his hopeful imagination was replaced with the dim one he has now. Ansley closes his eyes. He sees Connery growing old fast in a dive bar. Soon this plane will land and soon he will be driving about 100 miles. But not to Connery's farm. To her bar.

∾

Ansley hired a PI to keep an eye on Connery. Not a daily surveillance. More like monthly checkins. The first couple of reports were positive – they fit his imagination of a nature girl letting all the noise go and finding herself.

But then the third report came in. Connery was dating. A mostly out of work truck driver with a sick mother. This guy didn't seem to do much except suck up oxygen on Connery's serene farm. And yet she didn't push him away. He was *there* – there just like Alex had been *there*. Taking up her space and time. And she never insisted he give something back.

Something in Connery's heart lacks the strength to stop accidents like this from happening. Or perhaps, much to Ansley's horror – she wants the accident.

And the accident did happen. The sick mother got worse. Medical bills, rent, car payments – the mother couldn't pay for anything while getting cancer treatments.

Connery went thru the savings Ansley had given her in no time. And then one day the trucker floated an idea – just an idea: What if they sell the farm? They could have enough money to help his mother and also move into the city.

It went like that. The farm was sold. The sick mother took all the money. And she and the deadbeat trucker moved to the city. Life was loud again. Apartments were small again. And Connery is now a sweet bartender girl again, shacked up with a man she doesn't love and who will never leave her. Based on the surveillance photograph Ansley got, she is also starting to look her age. Even older. You grow old in a bar fast if it's the only place you can be alone in a crowd.

∼

ANSLEY HAS RENTED a nondescript Ford to follow Connery. He wants to see how she lives a typical day. Even though he already knows – but his heart has to see.

It isn't exciting. She appears to cook breakfast for the trucker and then take a nap with her two cats. At 4pm she awakes and showers quickly. And then she heads to Finnery's Cocktails. Which resembles Seashells in décor and drunks.

Once her shift at Finnery's is over, she heads out to a bar that stays open later than hers; she's found three. And she's still popular –

people, especially bar people, love Connery. They instinctively trust her and selfishly lean on her. And so she sits getting drunk while taking hugs of hello and talking about nothing. And when the bar closes she drunkenly drives home to the trucker. Screw or pass out, it's all the same. And then daylight comes and she does it all over again.

This surveillance makes Ansley so sad that he goes back to his hotel and gets plastered. He sleeps all day. He can't get out of bed. He can't stop thinking about what Randy said: "Do you ever think that God intended you guys to be with each other? And she might get lost all over again without you? That letting her go makes you a coward and a failure? Do you ever fucking think that maybe you needed that farm too?"

∼

IT IS JUST before close at Finnery's and Connery is counting money with her back turned to the bar. There are only two drunks left.

Finally Connery slams the register shut and turns around. Standing in front of her is Ansley. She gives him a smile for a moment, but his busted blue eyes erase it. And then it hits her: Ansley's here because he *knows*. He knows she lost the farm. He knows about the trucker. He knows every fucking thing.

Connery tries to speak but can't.

Ansley closes his eyes for a moment. He can't bear to see her like this. She can't stop making the same mistakes. She's an addict, addicted to bad decisions, to bad men who never will leave her because she's too good at keeping them. She willingly confuses being used with being needed. And an addict can only be true to their addiction, never themselves. When you look at an addict, you're looking at a lie.

Finally Ansley does open his eyes and sees Connery is crying. He wants to hold her and tell her he'll fix everything. But he can't. Life has moved on. He still loves her but his heart belongs to Siema now.

He had thrown money at Connery thinking it could fix her. Money can fix a lot in life but never an addict. Maybe his love could have. But he had let the moment go and moments have no encores.

Before Ansley turns to leave Connery mouths: I'm sorry.

Ansley manages to get to his car before he breaks down.

9

DETOUR LEANING

Ansley and Joey sit in a four star restaurant, Temptations. Known for steaks and seafood it also serves a helluva hamburger, which both of them order with fries. Ansley drinks beer. Joey drinks Coke.

This is a business lunch. Ansley knows that Joey helped Siema kill Gordon. Joey visited him several times in the hospital and his keen eye at reading people deduced something big had happened between them. He never mentioned his deduction to Joey.

Now that Gordon is gone, Joey's Deep State boss has taken over his interest in owning Clubland. Joey has suggested to him that the wealth of intelligence (re blackmail material) could only be improved if The Machine owned it thru a front company. This is Joey's big move and it is a smart one that will fast track him to the top.

"Nothing personal in this bud. But Clubland is just too much now. The Machine wants it and it could expose the real you. You can't fight The Machine bud."

"What is the real me Joe?"

Smiling, "The parts I took out of your background check."

"Yeah. So you really think that was the real me?"

"Yes I do. Beating a man to death is the real you. You got a sympathetic judge though."

"I turned 18 the day it happened. He decided that wasn't adult enough and cut me some slack. Plus there were mitigating circumstances."

"Two assholes raping a waitress in a fucking parking lot is definitely mitigating. And you just happened to walk by while it was happening and intervene. I call bullshit on that by the way."

Joey takes a bite of his burger and a sip of Coke. "I think you were sweet on the waitress. And you thought you'd show up at this club she liked to go to. And you watched her all night. Probably was sad when she left with two assholes. Lots of women get raped in parking lots. You were really fucking shocked when you saw what was going on weren't you?"

Ansley had felt dejected watching the waitress leave with the assholes. In truth she was just 20 and hadn't met a bad move she didn't embrace when it came to boys. Truth was it wasn't her first date rape. If Ansley hadn't been in puppy love with her he'd have realized sooner the danger she was in. Instead he sulked and this allowed for one of the guys to get off.

Ansley finally decided to bail once it was obvious she wasn't coming back, since there was no reason now to be in a loud club he hated. Upon exiting he saw the guy who got off first leaning on the waitress' car. Instantly he knew something was off.

The rest is fuzzy. He took out the leaning asshole with animal punches. He doesn't remember dragging the active rapist off the waitress. He can remember punching him though. He doesn't remember picking up that big rock and smashing his head.

Ansley's hatred of cruelty in the world makes him lose all control of his temper. He despises violence, physically can't stomach it – and yet when he sees cruelty in action, especially against women, he just loses it.

That night was over six years ago. It feels like sixty to him. At 18 he had a tiny opening in his orphan heart that hoped to find love with that poor waitress. And yet by 24 he had let Connery walk away as if it were a fait accompli. And it wasn't just Connery he had let go. There were others that he could have loved. But after that incident he decided that a poor orphan who trusts in romantic love is a dumb orphan. When it starts to feel real, it's really just a warning bell to let it go.

Ansley went to prison for fifteen months thanks to his sympathetic judge. He stumbled around after that and then one day he bumped into Benton Practice and just like that, Ansley Markus became Ansley Parade.

Ansley Parade never wants Siema to know what happened. He's sure she'd understand – she might even call him gallant. But he doesn't want the woman he loves to know he's capable of murder. The fact that she is also capable – whether directly or indirectly – does not strike him as equal. His murder was a frontal lobe misfire with some extra testosterone and orphan issues mixed in. Hers was a woman trying to save the man she loves.

Ansley smiles at Joey as he takes a bite of burger. This is Joe's poker move, he thinks. Since Joey hid Ansley's past he knows how desperate Ansley is to keep it hidden.

"This is your move huh? I don't cooperate and my past is suddenly prologue."

Staring down at his plate, "You owe me bud. For Connery. For that fucking tape I made disappear. Your whole game was made possible by me. You know how this works – quid pro quo. I told you from the start we're not friends."

Ansley reaches for his burger but suddenly doesn't feel hungry. "And if you are the point man on acquiring Clubland – that's a big feather in your hat."

"Very big."

Ansley is sure Joey has already promised his boss success. That means he will do whatever he has to do to pull this off. Death is rarely used by spooks. They usually prod and manipulate and cajole and blackmail their subjects. But death is on the list of tools to be used to make sure an "asset" cooperates.

Ansley searches Joey's eyes for friendship. He helped Siema plan

Gordon's death – hell he might have even done it. He wouldn't do that unless he cared for Ansley.

Or then Ansley thinks: Maybe Joey played the long game. Figuring that Gordon's exit would allow him to orchestrate Clubland's acquirement. A big get that will fast track Joey for upper management.

"What is it you want Joe? A simple sale?"

"No. We want you to publicly pretend to be involved. You're liked by the local press. We have a plan to publicly fix the Gordon mess. I mean you gave a press conference calling him a saint and he ends up a pedophile who ordered guys to kill you. But we can fix that."

"The Gordon storyline isn't as clear in the press as you've said it."

"Because we control the press Ansley. The ones we don't control we call conspiracy theorists. Fringe fuckers. Gordon was already using his power to quash it before –"

"He died unexpectedly." Ansley exchanges an intense glance with Joey. "From a heart attack."

So Ansley knows the truth, Joey thinks. He wonders if Siema betrayed him and confessed. He doesn't think so. He's known Ansley long enough to understand he's good at figuring out other people's shit.

"Sometimes Ansley you just get lucky."

Grinning, "We got lucky didn't we."

Joey's eyes go cold. "It doesn't matter Ansley. It always ends the same. The House wins. And the US Government is the House. You're going to sell."

A silence forms and they eat uncomfortably thru it for a while.

Ansley breaks the silence, "I assume it'll be a charity front."

"Of course. It's practically the same plan you announced for Gordon. On the surface anyway."

"You have no plans to give anything to my weirdos though."

"Ansley you're a dreamer. A dreamer makes good stories. Crazy anecdotes. He doesn't change fates."

"What about Jen and Randy?"

"They gotta go. Pay them off. Out of your own money. They're your responsibility."

Ansley drowns some french fries in ketchup. Has no intention of eating them. "When am I to announce it all?"

"Soon. That's all the calendar I have right now."

Ansley drowns some more french fries. He looks into Joey's eyes. Sees nothing. He wonders if Joey is the real Man Behind the Curtain. Gordon was pure evil but at least evil makes a choice. But Joey is pure practical – even if practical is a horror show.

Joey is going to be a problem because he places no bets and like the government he works for, comes out on top anyway.

~

ANSLEY IS DRIVING with a mind divided.

He wants Siema out of all this and the only way he can think of is to not tell her. But she's still a spook and likely will figure it out anyway. And he does not want to lie to her.

He could just sell. But what would happen to his ungrateful weirdos? And what would happen to Jen and Randy? Connery showed him that just giving people money does not fix troubled souls. Jen is bipolar and needs her time taken up in useful ways. Randy has managed to reach his mid-life crisis way early. Both need life to help them get to where they could be happy people. Money just handed over isn't life. It isn't purpose. Just the devil's tool used to destroy yourself.

Ansley will miss Clubland, but as an orphan he will always be wary of overstaying his welcome. And all he really wants now is to slow life down and be with Siema. Make a few babies who will never be orphans. And he's going to have to tell her his plan. She's both the only person he trusts to know it and also could help.

He pulls into his place now. Siema is in the barn cooking. He had arrived late last night back from his Connery visit. They both promised to talk over dinner.

Ansley walks in and sees Siema working on a meatloaf. She is wearing an apron because she knows he finds aprons sexy. She turns and smiles at him. "You look weird Ansley. What's up?"

Ansley takes a big, deep breath. He reaches in his pocket and gets down on bended knee, holding the small but elegant ring out to her.

"Siema Karim. Would you do me the honor of becoming my wife for the rest of my days?"

Siema's heart stops and then goes mad. Her hands are covered in the raw meat she is mixing for the meatloaf.

Ansley continues, "Please say yes Siema. I can't eat your meatloaf if you say no and I really want to eat your meatloaf. And let's finally say this out loud: I can't make love to you until we're married. And I really really really Siema want to make love to you."

He rises and grabs some paper towels, cleaning her hands. Siema then presses herself against his broad shoulders.

"I love you Ansley."

"I still don't hear a yes."

"Yes," she whispers.

"It does come with stipulations. One: I'll let you out of your yes if – after hearing my plan to get us out of this crap, you decide I'm a crazy fuck and want out.

"And two: We must get married tomorrow in front of a priest. I arranged one already – don't worry he won't be too upset if you back out because I already made a generous donation to his church.

"And three: I am an orphan with no family. But you're a Catholic Muslim – whatever the hell that is by the way – with a big one. We won't tell your family we got married without them. And I promise you a big big big white wedding with all of them eating and drinking when this is over. Well at least the Irish side can booze it up. The Muslims can eat all the non-pork, I guess.

"But I really need you *now* Siema. I need your help even though I don't want you involved. And I need you in my kitchen cooking meatloaf. And in my bed. In my arms. For the rest of my life. I love you and only you."

Siema can't control her tears. Ansley wipes them away. "I'll always do that for you," he says, "I promise."

Siema presses her head softly on his shoulder. "Tell me your fucked up plan while I finish the meatloaf."

∼

Once the meatloaf is done, Ansley explains his Connery visit.

Siema listens intently. She is not angry. She is wise enough to know you never own 100 percent of anyone's heart. And his loyalty to Connery both touches Siema and reconfirms that Ansley is kind and in the end, a life with him will be about kindness. Yes, he has demons and is capable of great violence. But if Siema's Catholic upbringing has taught her anything, it's that a man always has demons but he can, if his heart is right, overcome them.

However Siema is not just a Catholic. She's also a woman. So once Ansley is done explaining his visit to Connery she says, "Ansley you're a sweet kind man and I love you for not abandoning this girl. But you just put a ring on my finger. I expect to not hear her name again. You can't keep past loves anywhere but in the past. Are we clear?"

Ansley nods. He's thankful in so many ways that this signals the end of the subject.

"Ok," Siema says. "Now I am wearing white tomorrow in church. I don't care if no one will be there. No way I don't wear white in church when I marry."

∼

Clubland is unusually mad tonight. The street is holding a karaoke / dress like a rock star competition. There are Madonnas and Diana Rosses and Michael Jacksons and David Lee Roths and Axl Roses everywhere. Some of the singers are good – the short blonde girl dressed as Whitney Houston could actually sing like her. But most are David Lee Roth and Michael Jackson without the moves or pipes.

Ansley can take about five minutes of all this before it depresses the hell out of him. A check of his watch reveals it's time to hunt for Joey anyway. He should be at Club Insular.

Ansley walks into Insular's redecorated upper floor. It's filled with Christmas lights and clutter – except the clutter is pornographic and the waitresses are wearing Santa hats with dicks on them and little else. It kinda resembles Christmas by way of Satan.

Joey sits at the end of one of its bars sipping ginger ale. When he sees Ansley he smiles and waves him over. "Fun stuff they did here huh?"

Ansley nods. "It's very religious and traditional. Especially the dicks on the Santa hats."

"My tradition and religion is coked up party girls. So this place fucking rules."

"They landed on Plymouth Rock to give you this kind of religious freedom."

"So bud: You ok with everything? I really don't want any bad stuff between us."

Grinning, "I'm peachy."

Ansley noticeably moves his eyes toward a passing girl. "Hot damn the pusher man," he says.

Joey's eyes say hot damn the pusher man as well. This girl is a striking brunette with an ass that is both tight and has a poof, which her black vinyl pants show off stunningly. Her flowery blouse holds the tightest of breasts. Her smile is mischievous while her brown eyes twinkle under the Christmas lights. Ansley can see Joey is almost salivating. In a room full of hot coked up party girls, this chick *possesses* you. She is sex in motion.

Ansley leans in to block Joey's view and says, "Lena. That's her name. She's been taking Clubland by storm for about two weeks. Everybody wants her. Chicks and dudes."

Pushing Ansley out of the way to ogle Lena, "I am better than these other fuckers. I'm Joey motherfucker. Is she –"

"Seeing anybody? Like that would stop you. But man look at her! She enjoys the tease not the consummation. No one has gotten close."

Joey finishes his ginger ale. "Bud – I gotta go."

Smiling, "Religion will do that to you."

Joey heads off toward Lena. She is dancing the night away. Ansley can see Joey working up his best masculine pose. He thinks, Motherfucker does have righteous confidence with the chicks. I give him that.

Siema joins him now. They both lean against the bar while watching Joey cockily make his best pass.

"I suppose he has some charm about him," Siema says. "I still find him a cocky asshole."

"So do the chicks. They like fucking cocky assholes."

Grabbing his chin, "Not all chicks. When this is over I am gonna need you to tone done your cocky asshole."

"You know it's a bad idea to try and change your man."

Releasing his chin, "It's a bad idea to not change your man. My mother told me that when I was ten."

"I can't wait to meet her."

Siema grabs the fingers on his left hand. "I know we have to hide our marriage. But when this is over you better never take your ring off again."

Ansley grins at this. There is nothing better than a woman's jealousy to make you feel whole as a man. He grabs the fingers on her left hand. "And you better never take off yours."

"If I ever do Ansley that means you fucked up bad. Life won't be pleasant for you."

"Noted. How do you think Joey's doing?"

Smiling, "I think he thinks he's doing great."

∼

Lena scores some coke before she leaves with Joey. She doesn't tell him she's doing that. But of course he knows. But all Joey can think about is what her nipples look like. He couldn't care less what drugs she's into.

They take Joey's Bentley to her hotel. It's about ten miles away from Clubland. As they walk inside, Joey thinks her hotel is a bland, depressing place. But then he looks at Lena and nothing can be bland or depressing – this chick takes oxygen out of air.

Once in her small hotel room Lena wastes no time powdering her nose. She then walks out of the bathroom with a big smile and takes off her flowery blouse, revealing a tight red bra. And then she pushes Joey into the only chair in the room. Before he knows it she is in the throes of fellatio. He grabs at her incredible body. Life can't get any better than this.

And then the Vice squad busts in.

Lena screams and rolls away from Joey's crotch, leaving him half naked with a mighty erection and a gun in his face.

"I really really wish you were DEA," Joey says. "Then you might be in the wrong room."

∼

GETTING ARRESTED IS full of dead time and in the silence of it, Joey has been wondering if this bust is a freaky occurrence or if he's been setup. It's possible Lena just got ensnared in a bust when she scored the coke at the club. That would make him collateral damage.

Or it's possible Lena is collateral damage and he is the target. In any event his boss should be able to get him out of this predicament. He's given the cops the emergency number that will supposedly start the process of getting him out of jail.

Detective Lasser enters the interrogation room now. He is tall – about six feet four. Dark hair, dark eyes. He shaves every third day and this is only day two so his face is stubbly and rough. He's 35 but looks 45.

"So we called your boss," Detective Lasser says to Joey. He pulls out the paper that Joey wrote the emergency number on. "Strange thing is – the girl who was blowing you – she wrote the same number for us to call."

"What!" Joey screams. "I don't fucking follow you."

"Apparently she's your boss' daughter." Detective Lasser smiles. "And he's not happy with you."

∼

Siema phones Paul from a phone booth.

"Lena did great," she says.

Paul scratches at his bad hair. "We got lucky with daddy issues. She hates her father and so wanted to work for me if it meant working against his agenda."

Siema is amazed at Paul. How he got this intel on Joey's boss' family life, how he managed to recruit Lena without anyone knowing – he just had her on standby! Waiting for the perfect situation where her charisma and sexuality could knock it out of the park. Paul has moves all over the board just ready to go. He's a legit genius at the spy game. He may look like a badly dressed dork with bad hair – but don't fuck with him.

Siema suddenly thinks Paul's powerless appearance is just tradecraft, no more real than anything else they give you as pocket litter. It wouldn't surprise her if he really is a 6 foot 5 Adonis that she's been hypnotized into seeing as a short unremarkable dork.

"Paul – the girl did great tonight. But I worry about her holding up over the long haul. She won't tell her father the truth about you and us? Because it's juicy and it'll hurt him."

"Don't worry. She hates her dad but there is more to her than that. She's also young enough to wanna make a difference in the world. I explained how evil the world really is. How it's being run by sick guys like her father. When I told her this would embarrass and weaken him – I said it like she shouldn't do it – that's when her eyes lit up. I knew then she wouldn't fail us. And if she were to give us up, her dad could plot a win strategy. No way she wants her personal sacrifice to end up helping him."

"That makes sense," Siema says. "Joey was too easy in a way. As practical as he is about things, his dick isn't. A hot chick like Lena that no one could score? He just can't resist that."

"That detective you paid off to bust him was worth every penny. He really got the bust details out to the press fast. When Lena's dad saw her name and Joey's in the news concerning a club cocaine deal. Shit – he hit the fan! The official police report has been leaked to all our spy agencies. His daughter giving fellatio when the cops entered. He's a laughingstock. All the other spook CEO's are destroying him with jokes behind his back."

Siema can hear Paul's smile form as he says, "And Joey reached out to me last night."

~

Joey finds Ansley sitting on the same beach bench Julie and Ansley had used. It is 9am and Clubland sits with a hangover behind them.

Joey sits and says, "You fucked me bud. You really did."

Staring at the morning waves, "No. You fucked me. I ain't letting Clubland fall into The Evil Machine's hands."

"You use it for evil shit all the time!" Gesturing toward Clubland behind them, "Who the fuck cares about any of this in the end? It's just a passing fad. Why not just let it go?"

"I care Joe. I fucking care. This is my fucked up place and it's gonna stay a fucked up place where the weirdos inherit the earth."

"Those crazy fuckers – they don't even like you bud!"

"Outside of wait staff no one likes me Joey. And I buy their love. But Clubland is *mine*. Not yours or the fucking Evil Machine. Besides I think you're the real Man Behind the Curtain. You'll save my life or let thousands die. You'll feed a cat or kill a puppy – whatever's most practical to resolve a situation in your favor. You're really scary Joey. And I'd like to think you could be better."

"Fuck you."

Smiling, "Fuck me. You bet. But if I am right then there's something beyond selfish practicality in that heart of yours. And now working for Paul you might just find your better self."

Joey's boss wanted him fired. Actually he wanted him dead, fired was the compromise. Paul had managed to maneuver his way in with a unique trade. He said he had a compromised, and juicy, mission in Israel and would prefer to transfer that to Joey's boss, who once ran an Israeli station. If Joey's boss could fix it, it would be a big win that he desperately needs. In exchange he'd take Joey off his hands.

Paul never said that meant he'd also take Clubland off his hands. But since Joey's boss was distracted now – and Joey technically was still the designated point man on the deal for The Machine, all it took was speed to make sure his shell corporation bought Clubland instead of Joey's old boss'.

Ansley estimates they have about ten years before Paul will retire and the great Evil Machine will take over Clubland. But that's ok. No one wins forever. For now Jen and Randy and his weird business owners are safe. They will have some time to figure out life.

"I heard he's keeping you in Clubland," Ansley says. "So you get the beach, the babes, the Bentley I bought. Life's pretty good for ya Joe."

"I was heading toward being the next in line to run the show."

"Well maybe you'll run the show in Paul's neck of the woods. Provided you show him you have a heart and stop supporting evil because it's the most prudent choice."

"I don't know how you got his daughter.... It was Siema who came up with the plan wasn't it?"

"I had a good idea and she had some great ones. She is amazing Joe at plans. She has her dad's Muslim proclivity for exactitude. Doesn't that sound scary as hell by the way?"

"Oh fuck me."

"Siema is a helluva woman Joey."

"I can see why the club owners hate you Ansley. It isn't just the blackmails. You're worthy of being legitimately despised."

Ansley stands and Joey notices his wedding ring for the first time. "I'm off Joe."

He turns and looks at Clubland for a moment. It moves a little slow now under the morning sun. But still there's something about it, something simple and hopeful, something wild and free and strange.

Something the world usually crushes. He's going to miss it. He leaves fast so Joey won't see him tear up.

10

FIGHTING HORIZIONS

It is August, 2001. A lot has changed since 1994.
    A bit of history: Clubland was always going to be lost. But it took only five years, not ten, to lose it. Paul suffered a heart attack. Once he was buried the big Evil Machine took hold.

Jen was pushed out first. She didn't mind though. She had met a newly discharged army man in his early thirties who made her want to get pregnant. She has two kids now, boy and a girl, and likely will have more. As far as bipolar meds, she is still looking. But consenting to weekly therapy has helped. So has motherhood. It has made her focus and it's amazing how the mind can correct itself if it focuses.

Randy was also ready to leave Clubland. He went into political lobbying /consulting for so called "liberal causes." Ansley believes both are a form of legalized bribery. In any event he's found a man who works in politics to shack up with. Ansley assumes Randy is happy in the most unhappy way possible.

Joey extorted enough cash in his spook career that he didn't need a retirement fund. And when the Evil Machine took over, he too was ready to move on. Ansley had guessed right about Joey's heart. Working with Paul made him feel guilty about the sad world he was contributing toward. Once the Evil Machine took Clubland, Joey quit and became a fireman. He was always a man of action, he liked things to be intense. Plus chicks dig fireman and Joey will always need lots of chicks.

Ansley's weirdos lost everything. That was inevitable. Clubland was the only place in the world they had a chance. When the Evil Machine got it, they went back to being losers with even worse luck. It turned out sad but thanks to Ansley, for a little while, it wasn't sad. They had defeated the world. For a little while anyway. And that's about all anyone can ask for. To win for a little while and not have to sell your soul to get by.

Ansley is thinking about all this history today as he sits on a swing watching Siema plant flowers. She is five months along with their second child. The first, Aamira, named after Siema's grandmother, was born in 1997. Seeing her face for the first time is a moment Ansley relives often as he does farm chores.

For the most part they live off the land nowadays. They have only casual neighborly relationships. Both Siema and Ansley have trust issues outside of the family they've created.

But lately Ansley has been troubled. He can't shake a premonition that the world is about to explode. He's sure that something evil is in the air. Something the psychopaths will use to make the world less free and even more bloody.

And this bad mojo Ansley's sensing – he will fight to the death to keep his family out of it. Safe on this farm, far away from modern life and its fast paced psychopaths.

Ansley stopped dividing his life into albums once the Clubland drama was completed. The 24th was his last. And he stopped trying to live as if in a movie. Once he saw women as just pretty pop songs. But the two women in his life now, Siema and Aamira, are pop songs, concertos, symphonies and operas. They are simple and beautiful and complicated and sometimes, unknowable. His daughter inside Siema will be another mystery. The world is a large place, he thinks, but a man's heart is small. And this farm is the only world he cares to believe in.

Ansley walks over and takes Siema in his arms. "You know I

figured out just now what pop song you are."

"Which one?"

Ansley smiles and kisses her. "All of them," he says. "You've always been all of them and more to me."

Made in the USA
Columbia, SC
02 November 2024

7e12115b-f1a5-4017-acc5-3a44387bd8bcR01